Life Begins at Eighty

Annie Thompson

Acknowledgements

John, my husband, for reading the stories and letting me "hog" the computer.

Mr and Mrs Griffiths, my parents. Dad for inspiring"Going out with a bang" despite his safe driving and mum for patiently reading.

Aline Thompson, my mother-in-law, and Fred Laming her friend, for reading and support.

Christine Hayward, my patient beta reader, for her help and encouragement.

Karen Sabin, my school friend for some ideas, and reading and editing the stories.

Louise Thompson, also for ideas and reading.

Sarah Bennett, for taking time to help, although caring for a young baby.

Manoli Sánchez for help with the Spanish story and reading others.

Emma Foot for editing the stories and her sons Rowan and Isaac for reading.

Jeannie Abbott for her help and support.

Caroline Burgess, a local Ipswich artist, for her wonderful front cover design.

Naeem Kazi from Specsavers in Felixstowe for his support, and for the idea of my second book.

Ipswich Hospital for letting me photograph the display for "The Out of Date Shopping List".

George at Ipswich Station with his "table tennis bat".

Jamie at Felixstowe Leisure Centre with a detective game character!

Lily Tarbox for helping put it all together.

Felixstowe Scribblers for giving me some titles and ideas.

Contents

Loony Lorgnette (Speccles of Beccles)

In the corner of the well-loved optician's shop, Speccles, an elderly lady with a blue rinse twirled into an elegant bun sat reading a magazine, a tiny pair of pince-nez sitting at the top of her nose. For those of you who haven't heard of these before, they are tiny round eye glasses with no arms, that stay on your nose sometimes with a little spring clasp.

She had not been to the optician for many years now as she did not really trust optometrists since her previous one retired aged seventy plus, lived to be almost ninety and was no longer on the earth.

"Miss Kyson-Painter?" a softly-spoken gentleman approached the waiting people.

The lady looked up from her magazine delicately and pulled the eyewear from her nose.

"Eleanor Kyson-**Pointer** here "she said in a timid but well–educated voice.

The gentleman, perhaps in his thirties, beckoned her to one of the rooms at the back where eyes are tested.

"How are you?" he enquired."I am Nadeem." He shook her hand.

"Oh, not so bad, thank you. I'm just not seeing so well. I expect it's my age."

"We'll see how your prescription has changed, and sort you out with something maybe more modern?"

"Oh, I don't think I could cope with anything too modern." The lady smiled nervously and sat in the special chair he had beckoned her towards.

She sat at the machine with her chin on the rest and peered at the selection of dots she had to look at.

"Where are the frames that you slot lots of lenses into?" She demanded of the gentleman who tested her eyes.

"Those are all in the past. It's all done with computers now," he chuckled. "Now, which is clearer, number 1 or number 2?"

"Oh, it's so difficult! They are both quite clear. Can't you give me some letters to read?"

The gentleman showed her some letters ahead of her, and she was barely able to read any below the second line.

"Before I send you to see about new lenses we need to check the pressure of your eye", he announced. Would it be all right to puff a tiny amount of air into your eye?"

"Well, I dare say you could have a go, if you must". Well, she jiggled around in her seat, turned her head around and "PUFF!" A tiny whoosh of air went into her right ear.

"Oh, I'm so sorry! I am training to be an audiologist, but that was meant to go in your eye!" The friendly optician tried to make light of the problem, but Miss Kyson-Pointer was very embarrassed.

"One more try", she suggested. However, the puff of air gave her such an unpleasant surprise she blinked and jumped, and she had to give up on the test.

"I'm so sorry, I can't have any more of this poppycock!" she exclaimed. The gentleman who helps choose frames, Oliver, then knocked on the door.

A friendly chap with glasses himself, Oliver tried his hardest but found it very difficult to advise her on a new type of eyewear that was suitable for her new prescription.

"I haven't had a new prescription in thirty years plus, and I'm not starting on spectacles NOW, at my age. Can't I just have the new lenses put in this frame?"

"I'm afraid, madam, they don't make those any more. They only sit on your nose. It must be very difficult to keep them on. You need something to wrap round your ears."

Miss Kyson-Pointer looked horrified at this.

"Keep them on? I can't do that, dear. I only use them when I go to the theatre or the opera, or read my book. I have sensitive ears, so I don't want bits of wire or plastic wrapped round them. That's all nonsense to me."

"But how do you drive? It must be very difficult with those little specs clipped painfully to your nose?"

"Indeed I do not drive. I ride my bicycle. It's a *Wayfarer,* I had it in the seventies."

"Well, Miss Kyson-Pointer, we have an offer on your lens. Two pairs for the price of one. You can choose very lightweight sides. They aren't like in the old days, pressing on your ear. It would be so much easier for when you ride your bike."

"Oh but I only need ONE pair, surely you can do me some sort of deal? And I *don't need them to ride my bicycle!*"

Another member of staff, Petra, a willowy young lady just out of college, overheard Oliver's conversation with the older lady.

"Sorry to be ear-wigging, but how about having one side, a sort of lorgnette? You could at least hold them to your eyes, and move them nearer or further away as necessary."

"Now that's a splendid idea. I will consider that. Thank you so much for your help."

"What sort of colour would you like? Your lenses have a tiny silver frame. Would you like a silver arm to match?"

"Well to be honest, I rather fancy a pebbledash effect. Is there such a thing?"

"I'm sure we could sort that" Oliver decided. He found her an arm she liked, and tried to measure where the centre of her pupils would be in the new lenses. He drew little specks for the centre, roughly where he thought the middle of her eyes would be. Of course it was very difficult, as it would depend how near or far away she was holding the arm.

"I won't have dots on my new lenses, will I?"

"No, I just need to make sure they're properly centred. Now, can you read this line for me?" He held the lenses to her eyes.

"Books printed on very large papers and having money works...."(*printed on large pages and having many words*)

"Navels and aubergines...." (The sentence was actually "*Novels and magazines....")*

Oliver was baffled. He didn't remember a line about navels, and that other sentence didn't sound right. What on earth was he going to do with this customer? He gave her a hand-held board with some very simple sentences, and fortunately she could read every one.

"Your lorgnette will be ready in ten days" Oliver told her, "I will arrange to see you myself. Have a good few days" he beamed.

Well, on March the fifth she returned to pick up her special lorgnette. She was quite excited about the prospect.

"I'm so sorry, Miss Dyson-Pointer. I have no case big enough to fit your new eyewear," Oliver greeted her.

"Ah, I have brought one with me. My grandfather left it to me. And it is Kyson, not Dyson. I have nothing to do with the scoundrel who invented a modern vacuum cleaner."

She sat at the desk with Oliver and held the new lorgnette to her eyes.

"What line can you read here?" He held up a card with snippets of various poems on them, and he held the lorgnette for her.

"I can only see a couple of tins of baked beans and a coffee jug over there."

Oliver didn't know what on earth she was talking about. He glanced round to see what she could possibly be looking at. There was a sort of tube in the corner, where they could send glasses up to the first floor in tubular plastic cases. (They called this the *Whoosh Tube*). If looking from a distance, you could possibly think the bottom of the tube was a coffee jug. The tubes themselves were green, but not quite the right colour for baked beans?

"Ah, my dear, I fear you're looking a bit too far away. Here, read these for me." He held the poetry a few inches from her nose, and she seemed to manage to read it.

"I could do with a cup of coffee," she announced. "You've worn me out with that reading!"

"I'm ever so sorry. You'll have to go to the cafe next door for coffee, but I can get you some water if you like." He explained about the Whoosh tube and how the cylinder does indeed look like a coffee jug. She giggled nervously.

"How silly I am! Never mind, I'll be fine now thank you. I'll be using these now whenever I can. Thank you so much", and she shook Oliver's hand and swept elegantly out of the shop, the lorgnette safely in the case she had brought. I say she swept, as she was wearing a long cape.

Well, she got home, made herself some tinned tongue salad with bread and butter, and settled down to read her newspaper. Poppet the cat sat on her usual chair looking very regal, sitting in sphinx position, licking her paws as she'd been given a few bits of tongue. Eleanor read a few headlines, but the words made no sense at all. It looked as though the Duchess of Cambridge was being reflected in a pool of water, and all the Arsenal players seemed to be standing on their heads. What on earth was going on in the world? Mind you, the American president did look better how he was, in a blur of mist. She then fell asleep, as she occasionally did after trips out on her bicycle.

When she woke, the new lorgnette was on her lap. She picked it up and looked over to where the cat had been sitting. The poor cat was upside down!! "Oh, my giddy aunt," muttered Eleanor to herself. "I fear another trip to Speccles is on the cards."

She telephoned her friend Doctor Roy Burrows, so called as he had gained a PhD many years ago, though (some may say) not in any useful subject and he now lived in Sheltered Accommodation on the same side of town as she did.

"How the devil are you, darling?" he boomed down the telephone (which incidentally was an old style one, where you turn a dial instead of pressing numbers as you can buy retro ones these days.)

"I'm having a frightful time with my new lorgnette" she said. "The people in the news are all upside down and so is Poppet!"

"Are you holding it the right way up, sweetie?"

"Of course I am!"

"Well, take the darned thing back, and see the manager!" was Roy's reply." In actual fact, I need a hearing test. Do they do those? I can hear you now on the telephone, but last week every time my son sneezed, I thought it was a dog barking, and when next-door's baby cried I thought it was a seagull. Most disturbing."

"Well, my optician said he was training to be an audiologist, so you could see him. He was very gentlemanly."

"Right-oh, old girl. I'll ring them in the morning."

The following morning came, and they went together to the optician. The doctor strode along, and Eleanor in her cape trotted along beside him.

"Well, Mrs Kyson-Pointer! I'm sorry you're having trouble. I'll be with you in a few minutes." Dr Roy went to see an audiologist (a fully qualified one, not the gentleman Eleanor had seen previously) while Eleanor waited in the corner. She took her lorgnette out of its case and it steamed up immediately.

"Gosh, are you here for steamed up lenses?" asked a large young blonde lady in a broad Essex accent. Eleanor laughed.

"Ah, there's a bit more to it than that," she said shyly.

"It seems to be missing an arm; there should be more to it!"

"No, it's meant to be like this. How about yourselves?"

"We came up from Tilbury. Couldn't get an appointment at Speccles there. This one is well-known for being friendly," the friend, brunette and smiley, informed her.

Oliver then came over to collect Eleanor.

"What's going on then?"

"Well, and I'm *Miss* ....you called me "Mrs" earlier... I don't know if it's my age or..."

"Hold it to your eyes, please," Oliver gestured towards the lorgnette.

She picked it up and ..

"OH! I think I know the problem! I'm so sorry, it's my fault. I've just realised you're left-handed and the arm is the wrong way, as we wrongly assumed you were right–handed."

"Thank Goodness I'm not going mad!"

"As compensation we will do you a spare, as well as sorting this one; just tell me what colour arm you'd like".

"A spotty design would be lovely," Eleanor beamed.

"And you can have a cup of coffee made in our staff kitchen." He unfortunately couldn't send the lorgnette upstairs in the little cylinder via the Whoosh tube as it was too long, but he got a cup of coffee for her while she waited for Dr Roy.

Well, Dr Roy was having trouble hearing the lady audiologist who had a soft voice. She asked him to sit closer to the machine, and he heard "Toaster machine", and told her no, he made his toast under the grill every morning. She then asked him to put up his hand every time he heard a noise from the machine in his ear. However he heard the word "stand" and so tried to stand when he heard a squeak, and hit his head on the coat hook.

"I'm going to order you a hearing aid for both ears," she said in a louder voice at the end.

"What will they be made of?" enquired Dr Roy.

"High tech plastic. You won't know they're there."

"Oh, I can't have that. They must be ear trumpets. Made from shell. I prefer a seashell to a snail shell, if you don't mind."

The audiologist thought the old chap was joking. Maybe in the old days, the aids were made from shells but not now, surely?

"Great! I'll get two from the beach, I live right next to Lowestoft," she giggled, to humour him.

"I say, that's awfully kind of you. I would much prefer those in my ears."

The two elderly folk set off home, Eleanor carrying her pince-nez for temporary use and the doctor mishearing her.

Another ten days later they had a call from Speccles, and they hurried along to collect a pair of wonderful hearing aids made with seashells and a lorgnette with the arm on the left side. Now and then they got themselves in a muddle and Eleanor would pop his ear trumpets into her ears to try to help her see better and he would pop on her lorgnette, upside-down of course as he was right – handed, to help him hear better.

Well, those of you who wear glasses must admit you have sometimes cleaned them so you can hear more clearly?

The Unusual Gifts

Dr Roy's grand-daughter, Daisy, who was a yoga teacher, had just had a baby boy. She had never seemed a maternal type, and her husband Sam, an artist, didn't really seem practical enough to manage children. Mind you, Daisy thought nothing of getting up at five in the morning to do a "salute to the sun", and was a healthy eater. No one would have ever known she was pregnant, because she remained very slim, and because she always wore yoga pants which looked like "harem trousers", her "baby bump" had been well–disguised. Many of the family members had a complete shock when they heard of Toby's birth.

Well, Dr Roy was wondering what on earth he could get as a gift for the new baby. He consulted his friend Eleanor Kyson-Pointer. She used to belong to a knitting group and still kept in touch with a much younger lady who made lovely little knitted shoes. Admittedly they would only fit the baby for a couple of months, but then again so did most baby clothes. When they chose them they couldn't remember if the baby was a boy or a girl, so they chose an olive green pair which could be suitable for either. They were wrapped in lovely tissue paper and the Dr then put them in a little gift bag ready for when he went to visit.

The day before, he couldn't find the little gift. He rang Eleanor, hoping she had it at her place.

"Eleanor dear, what happened to the little boots? I can't find the packet."

"What did it look like, Doc?" (Eleanor often called him "Doc".)

"Well I'm sure it was wrapped in tissue and then put into a little gift bag," he said, hoping that was right.

"I'll go and look, and get back to you." She went off to look in her spare room, where there were all sorts of items. Unwanted presents she had received, gifts she had for other people but not yet given, items belonging to her parents from years ago, and sewing patterns, newspaper cuttings and goodness knows what else. Her eyes alighted on a little gift bag with a poodle on the front, and when she went to feel it something soft was inside it in tissue paper. She rang the Doctor immediately;

"I think I've found your packet," she announced.

"What jacket d'you mean, sweetie?" he boomed.

"PACKET, the baby gift. Has a dog on the bag."

Dr Roy couldn't remember a dog, but was sure it would be right, and he didn't have time to go out shopping now. He met Eleanor to pick it up the next day. Soon afterwards he travelled with his daughter to see the new baby. He was a handsome little chap, as babies go, smiling away and listening to the "whale" music Daisy was playing on a CD. Well, Roy's daughter Pauline had bought most of the items for the nursery, so he was a little embarrassed handing over a small gift bag with a poodle on.

Daisy peeped inside and pulled out an item wrapped in lovely tissue paper.

"Ooh, Toby. What have you got here? She opened the tissue paper with one arm round Toby who was in his little bouncy chair. Imagine everybody's surprise when out came a silky scarf, in mauve, with a bottle of "Old Norfolk lavender" spray falling out onto the floor.

"Oh,Toby! Do you like lavender? It's very good for sleep and healing, but -and a lovely soft scarf...I fear this is for someone else.. granddad, but thank you; it's the thought that counts..."

"Daisy sweetie, there's been some sort of mistake. Don't worry; I'll get the right present to you as soon as I can."

They all sat and had tea and cake, and Daisy fed Toby who then went for a lie–down. Doctor Roy was embarrassed at having to take the present away again but assured Sam and Daisy he would sort the confusion as soon as he could. When he got home he scoured his lounge for any wrapped gifts but could not find any.

A couple of days later he went over to Eleanor's house to see if he could solve the problem there. She had just had a phone call inviting her to her friend Hermione's 85th birthday party the following week. "I'm sure I had a gift sorted, and it's not here. Maybe it's at yours?" The doctor had forgotten to bring the lavender gift back that day.

"I don't think so, but I'll look when I get home" the Dr reassured her. He didn't have as much "clutter" as she did in her house but he did have a shed stuffed with all manner of DIY equipment from jars of screws and nails, hammers, step ladders; not to mention parts of old bicycles, although he didn't actually own a whole bicycle.

In the meantime they scoured her spare room, and after going through many of the items of her parents, all bagged up, and the unwanted gifts, such as handbags she intended to pass on.

Eventually they came across a little gift bag in a pastel orange colour. However at that moment the 'phone rang which distracted Eleanor; she went to answer it leaving the Dr searching through some items. He eventually found an old cigarette case and holder wrapped in tissue paper.

When she came back from the telephone she was a bit flustered as she'd got the window cleaner's dates in a jumble and he was away the week she needed him. So they had a cup of tea and Dr Roy showed her the cigarette case.

"Actually, as I can't find Hermione's gift I may give her this, she occasionally smokes and she loves old things. You'd best take the orange packet, which must be for the baby."

Well, they thought they had the right packages, and off went the Doctor at eight o'clock after crumpets and jam.

The following Wednesday Miss KP put on her best clothes and went to Hermione's for tea, armed with a gift.

Hermione was quite an outgoing old lady, who used to be on the stage, mainly amateur dramatics." Eleanor, how absolutely wonderful to see you. How well you look. Come and give me a big kiss," She opened her arms out to Eleanor.

"Hello sweetie, you don't look anywhere near eighty-five," said Miss KP in flattering tones. She handed over the gift, which Hermione ripped open with excitement. Inside was, indeed you've guessed it, a pair of gorgeous knitted olive baby shoes!!

"Oh, Eleanor! What have we here? Please don't say you're going senile, old girl. I'm too old to have a baby, and have no youngsters in the family, but I'm sure you bought these for someone with a baby."

"Oh!" exclaimed Eleanor. "Indeed, they were for Dr Roy's great grandchild. How frightful, I'm so sorry. I think we've been giving people the wrong gifts as they were in similar little bags. You will get your present in the end".

However, the very next day, Dr Roy had the chance of meeting up with Daisy and Toby in a department store cafe, and as well as buying some items of clothing for Toby he decided to hand over what he hoped was the right present. They had just settled Toby in his little travel-carrycot and finished a pot of tea and some delicious cheese scones.

"Here's your gift you should have had the week before last; sorry it's late. Eleanor's friend knitted them herself." He handed over the gift bag, which he thought should have been orange, but anyway it felt soft.

Daisy took the peach-coloured item and undid the sellotape. Inside was an item very well - wrapped in tissue paper. Then, to Daisy and the Doctor's amazement, out came a tiny silky bag containing a stainless steel slim case that looked like a very flat diary. "Oh, what have we here?" asked Daisy with a smile. She shook out the tissue paper and out slid a long slim silver article, cylindrical, less than half an inch in diameter.

"OH NO!" cried Dr Roy. "Eleanor's cigarette holder and case; she was going to give them to Hermione. Oh my Goodness, you must think I'm quite a nutcase."

"Well, you are my grandfather, and quite a fine old age. These are the funniest knitted things!! I really don't want Toby to start smoking at an early age, especially with me being a yoga teacher."

"Poor Hermione must have got Toby's gift for her 85th!!"

The saga of the gifts couldn't be resolved for another few months, as Hermione went into hospital. She was under strict orders not to smoke again, but she agreed to keep the case and holder as a little keepsake, and loved her lavender items too. Dr Roy got the little shoes to Daisy but Toby was by then nearly a year old and toddling around.

"I'm afraid you may have to keep these for your next baby. I'm so glad we didn't get a boyish pair," he apologised to Daisy.

"I'll let you into a secret," she whispered. "I'm expecting again, and they are gorgeous little shoes for a boy or girl. They will certainly come in handy in a few months' time!"

The Cape

We have already met Eleanor Kyson-Pointer, who was an elderly lady, maybe in her early eighties, and had long silver hair (sometimes tinged with pink) twirled into a neat little bun, with pins sticking out in all directions. She lived in a small Suffolk town, and often travelled by bicycle, and she had a gentleman friend, Dr Roy Burrows, who lived in a sheltered accommodation scheme on the same side of town.

This lady had a cape in which she sort of swept around. She'd had it since the 1970's, and had made it herself from a large piece of green checked material and as it wasn't very thick, she had made a red fleecy lining to go inside in the winter. She sewed the lining in three or four places in the winter and unpicked it in summer.

Miss KP had a firm dislike of modern things. She couldn't bear microwave ovens, mobile telephones, and anything to do with satellite navigation. Her particular dislike one year was of banks. They were always trying to ask her if she'd like online banking or to upgrade her account. She got so cross about all this, as well as with the rather smarmy bank manager, that she decided to take her pension out in huge wads of money and then store it in the house. She didn't want to be one of those funny people who stitched banknotes into the mattress or the curtains but had an idea that she could stitch some of the money into the lining of her cape. She would have to then stitch the lining in all along the hem and not just in places. In the spring when she took the lining out she would open an account at another bank or think what else to do.

Well, at the end of November she had a dreadful case of toothache. She was quite partial to having a cake in the afternoon, and although she had brushed her teeth very regularly she was now in her eighties and teeth just don't really last that long.

"I'm so sorry," Mr Ferretti the dentist said. "I'm going to have to remove six or seven teeth and have some dentures made for you, sort of half a top set". He measured her up and gave her a rough estimate of four hundred pounds. When she went back a week later she took her friend Dr Roy Burrows, who usually helped her on health appointments when he could. Eleanor wasn't a great one for medical appointments and was quite nervous about the whole procedure.

"I think it's quite preposterous that you should have to pay to have teeth removed" her friend Dr Roy claimed.

"Well at least with the new teeth I'll be able to chew my food again, and speak more clearly", Eleanor said.

On the allotted day Roy's brother Dean, who happened to have an old car, offered to drive her, and Dr Roy came too. Miss Kyson-Pointer was a bit squeamish about having injections in her mouth, so she had been practising yoga breathing, taught to her by Dr Roy's grand-daughter.

Well the traumatic part was over and she had a big gap in her teeth where seven teeth were missing. The problem now was she was going to have to eat soft food for a while until the new teeth were ready and she was having trouble speaking, or rather Doctor Roy, who was hard of hearing, was having trouble understanding her. He had a pair of hearing aids, which were made from shells, as like Eleanor, he disliked modern items and couldn't bear plastic in his ears. On this occasion, he wasn't wearing them.

"My new teeth will be ready in a week," she rang him as soon as she heard.

"Did you say we're having beef next week? My favourite, with Yorkshire Pud."

Eleanor despaired. "I said my TEETH will be ready in a week. Once I'm used to them we'll have roast beef."

"Oh, sorry, old girl. Of course, you need to sort your teeth first. Let me know and Dean, so we can all go and collect them."

The teeth were ready on the Tuesday and off they trundled, squashed in the old car. Incidentally, Dean's car would only go up to third gear or it would judder, so there was a lot of hooting, and drivers making fists at them, but none of the passengers noticed. They rattled along to a quiet village nearby, where the dentist was.

"Hello there, Miss Kyson-Pointer", beamed Mr Ferretti. "I have your new teeth; I hope you'll like them."

"Goodness me!" Eleanor exclaimed, as she looked at the teeth which were new-looking but fortunately not gleaming white. Mr Ferretti had fortunately matched them to her remaining teeth. "I was going to pay you first. Here, let me find my cheque book." She rummaged in her handbag where there were all manner of items. These included her new lorgnette in its special case from her grandfather (Miss Kyson-Pointer disliked spectacles), a few mints, some tissues which were now looking scruffy, and a bottle of

English lavender perfume. No cheque book, or even a wallet or purse. She stared at the dentist in horror.

"Don't worry," said Mr Ferretti. "We'll sort the teeth first, and think after".

Whilst in the dentist's chair, Miss KP had a thought. She had obviously forgotten her cheque book, and wallet, but of course! She had some money in the lining of her cape. How could she get it without anyone seeing? Should she sneak into the toilet? But wouldn't she need a pair of scissors? It was quite embarrassing; she had a large chunk of her savings in there and it may all fall out at once.

"Miss Kyson-Pointer! Are you OK? Would you like some tea?" a voice enquired. She must have fainted either from the embarrassment, or just the thought of the missing teeth, and she felt all woozy.

"A cup of tea would be nice, oh and erm – could I have a pair of scissors?" Mr Ferretti and his nurse looked at one another in amazement.

What did she want those for? "I seem to have a bit of a knot, and I need to cut it. Could you pass my cape over?"

The dental assistant (Aggie) passed the cape over and a pair of scissors, and Eleanor began to feel all round where she'd sewn the lining inside the cape. She felt a chunk of banknotes and so snipped away.

"Here's your tea, I've put it by the basin where the pink water usually sits!" A voice beside her jolted her and she jumped, so of course several bundles of twenty pound notes jumped from her lap onto the floor. Aggie tried to pick some up, and Eleanor squealed as she tried to block the gap in the lining, but more notes fell out in bundles and they went under the dentist's desk, his lamp, and everywhere.

"Oh, it's like a party game!"laughed Mr Ferretti. "You don't owe me quite this much. Here, we'll count it out together. He counted out the three hundred and sixty pounds in twenty pound notes - as it was slightly less than he'd said - and then they recovered all the bundles from the floor and put them into an envelope for her. Aggie fortunately happened to have a needle in her handbag and some cotton, and sewed the small hole in the cape lining while Eleanor drank her tea.

When Dr Roy heard the story, he laughed. "You don't want to lose all your money going over bumps in Dean's rickety old car!"

Dean himself suggested Eleanor should get herself along to another bank as soon as possible to open another account; maybe the Post Office wouldn't badger her into online banking or posh new accounts. At least she enjoyed chatting to all the staff in there.

Every time she visited the dentist, she made sure she wore a different coat or jacket, but they still asked what had happened to her cape!!

The Treasure Trove

Eleanor and Dr Roy had many hobbies in common, which is why they got on so well. They often went on little trips together, whether to the seaside, town, or just somewhere for a cup of tea. One Tuesday in autumn they decided to go to their favourite second–hand bookshop, which seemed to specialise in train books and local history books. Eleanor particularly liked historical fiction and the Dr enjoyed crime writing and thrillers. They decided to catch a bus into town as they each had a bus pass. First they went to the country market, where they each bought some eggs and fresh vegetables, and they decided to have a spot of lunch there. They then ambled, at the Dr's slow but steady pace, with Miss Kyson-Pointer trotting along next to him, down to The "Treasure Trove".

This looked quite a small shop from the front when you stood outside it, but when you went inside it went a long way back. It was stuffed full of books on every subject under the sun, all second-hand, including those mentioned above, and ranging from fiction through cookery to fly fishing, with a children's section and a large philosophy section. There were corridors leading this way and that, little nooks and crannies, and little doors here and there saying "Staff only" or "Sorry no entry this way". There were a few armchairs dotted around, and often older ladies and gentlemen with spectacles were sitting reading entire novels there, and spotty youths were looking at books with naked ladies in.

The lady and gentleman who ran the bookshop, a friendly couple from the north of the country, often offered cups of tea or coffee to members of the public who often bought items or liked to pop in often. The youths would jump when the staff went past, in case they knew their families, which in many cases they did, but as they tried to pretend they were looking at something else a cheery voice would ask "Cup of tea?" On one occasion, after hearing this a young man who was standing dropped a large book about Fly Fishing which was hiding "The Joy of Sex part 2"and was so embarrassed he left the shop, scattering books in all directions.

"Hello there, Miss KP and Dr Roy!" called the lady, Heather, on this particular occasion.

"Hello", replied Eleanor taking her lorgnette out of its case and peering more closely at a book behind Heather entitled "The life and habits of weasels".

"Yes, we do have some bizarre titles," smiled Heather. "Is there anything you're looking for? I have an entire shelf devoted to pigeons."

"I'm looking for a book on the rules of the universe, by MJ Pinkerton" announced the Dr, "and I will have a look at the crime novels. I love Agatha Christie and her followers."

"And I'm just going to potter about, if that's OK". This was Eleanor, now peering through the lorgnette at some wartime magazines preserved in plastic wallets.

"I'll bring you some tea around three, is it still milk and half a sugar each?"

"Yes, thank you," they said in unison.

Well, they each settled in an armchair, quite near to one another, with a pile of books each.

They were brought a cup of tea at three, and then some time before four the Dr paid for a couple of Agatha Christie books and a railway jigsaw. However Eleanor hadn't found anything she fancied, so she went deeper into the shop, right near the back, to look at some recipe books written by a mature blonde lady cake maker who seemed to have made a return to the television screens. She found a book from 1970 and was intrigued by it especially as the lady was around her age.   However as she was rather tired, she dropped the lorgnette she'd been holding, onto the book, and fell asleep.

It was almost five when the Doctor ambled slowly towards the back of the shop, stopping to peer at some interesting articles about train timetables from the "fifties", when he finally caught sight of Eleanor on a sofa in a most unladylike pose, snoring with her mouth open, her cape open beneath her, a large cookery book on her lap and the lorgnette balanced precariously.

"Eleanor my dear!" called Roy."I fear the shop may be closing soon."

Miss Kyson-Pointer woke with a start. She couldn't think where she was, but certainly there was no Poppet the cat meowing for her breakfast. "Where are we?"

"We're in The Treasure Trove, and I think we need to get out quite soon. It must be closing soon. It's twenty past five."

"Oh my Goodness, yes, I need to be getting home."

They gathered their belongings and set off towards the front of the shop, both worrying they couldn't see anyone at all on the way. Imagine their horror when they got to the door and it had a sign with "OPEN" facing them, meaning one thing; the "CLOSED" sign was on the outside. What on earth were they to do? Dr Roy pushed and pulled the door in the hope that there was some mistake, but no, it was most definitely locked.

"Well, Eleanor. Do you want me to call the police?"asked Roy, worriedly.

"We don't even have a mobile telephone," said Eleanor in a weak voice.

"We can use their phone, old girl."

"Well to be honest, I don't want to cause anyone any trouble. I can quite easily sleep on that sofa, as you saw."

"Yes, indeed. Don't you take tablets though; won't you need them?" The Dr remembered a time when they had thought she may be diabetic.

"No, remember I only take vitamins and calcium. How about you?"

"Well, I should take my thyroid tablets, but I reckon I'll be OK as long as we can leave first thing in the morning. "

"What if it's early closing tomorrow?"asked Eleanor, worried again."I can't leave poor Poppet 'til Thursday."Dr Roy looked through the glass door and was able to read the days of opening, Tuesday to Saturday. He'd been sure the shop was only closed Sunday and Monday.

"Don't forget, dear, we have carrots, leeks and eggs!" announced Dr Roy, "But I don't know if there are any cooking facilities."

"We'd better have a nose through some of those doors, to check for a closet, and some sort of kitchenette. They've clearly got teabags here. I'm sure we'll survive."

They pottered along back to the first door that was labelled "Staff Only". The Dr pushed the door. Oh no! It was locked! Should they go and find the telephone, and ring Heather or her husband? Or try the other door? Eleanor rested on a chair, and the Dr went to the next door.

This was also locked, but high up on a little hook was a set of keys. Aha! Would he be able to open both doors with this key? Was there a light? It was getting dark outside and the shop was quite poky; he would need to put a light on. Would the police think they were burglars then? Oh dear, it didn't bear thinking about!!!

Actually, the shop was long and narrow, so unless they had the light on by the door, no one would even see a light from the street. Dr Roy felt in his inside jacket pocket and found the slim torch his son had given him last Christmas. He could see sufficiently to try the keys on the hook, and amazingly one was to the one door, which led to a kitchenette with another door to a small toilet and wash basin. He checked the room and realised there was a microwave oven as well as a kettle, and some milk in the fridge. Dr Roy was not a fan of microwave ovens and would not have one in his house, and neither was Eleanor, but his daughter and her family raved about eggs and potatoes cooked in them. They would be fine with a cup of tea now each and some scrambled egg, and a cup of tea in the morning. He went to find Eleanor to tell her of his finds. She was sitting on a comfortable armchair studying a recipe.

"Would you like a scrambled egg, my dear?"

"Oh, yes please, but I suppose there's no hob", came the reply.

"Don't worry. I can investigate the microwave. Beastly modern things, but needs must."

He rustled up a very nice snack, as he found some bread to toast, (and decided he would replace it the next day), some butter, and a pot of tea in a dear little teapot from the cupboard. He served it up on a tray, and they sat eating it on an armchair each, with a coffee table he found near the geography books.

After she had eaten, Eleanor yawned and said, "Would you mind awfully if I sleep on that sofa again? I feel exhausted."

"Not at all. I'll give you my overcoat, and I'll rummage around and see if I can find any blankets."

He found the door he hadn't tried yet, still with his torch, and with one of the keys he managed to open it. It led to a spiral set of stairs, which the Dr didn't really fancy climbing, but thought he should check for something to cover his friend. He didn't want her becoming poorly now she was eighty-two.

At the top was a funny little office. There was a light switch to the right, and once it was on he saw the room overlooked the backs of houses and a passage between the bookshop and a sort of modern food outlet, so he kept his head down to avoid being seen. There was a desk with a computer on, and piles of papers listing books in orders of subject, author name and Goodness Knows what. Stationery of all kinds sat on the table, pens, scrap paper, treasury tags, paperclips, sellotape, and you name it; it was there. The telephone was here too, and a list of numbers, but he didn't see Heather's name on the list.

There was a cupboard to one side which he opened, but alas, there were no blankets there. It only contained boxes of ancient jigsaws, magazines, "Airfix" models in tattered boxes, and a few ancient music cassettes.

On the way back down, he noticed another cupboard, under the stairs. It was difficult to open as something was stuffed inside. He pulled it, and it was a duvet!! The doctor disliked these items with a vengeance, as you couldn't take one on or off, like a blanket, with duvets, to make yourself warmer or cooler, but this time he was happy to see it. In fact there were two single ones, one thick and one thin, and a couple of pillows. They seemed to have brightly coloured covers, and were dusty, but he didn't mind.

As he passed the kitchenette, Eleanor came out of the toilet with her bun undone, hairpins in hand. She also had taken out her new partial set of teeth, and gave him a funny sort of smile.

"Oh, look what you've found!"she enthused. "Sorry I can't thpeak much now," she lisped.

"Not to worry, you have a good rest. We'll get you home tomorrow."The Dr smiled and carried the thicker bed cover all the way to the back of the shop to Eleanor's sofa. He went back for his, settled in the comfiest armchair, took out his special shell hearing aids, and settled back into the chair.

Once those were out he couldn't hear a thing, and considering he wasn't on a bed he had a good sleep.

The following morning the Doctor, who was nearer to the front of the shop than Miss KP, was sure he could smell bacon.

"Where am I?"he wondered. He was sure he wasn't in a bed and breakfast place, and didn't usually bother to do bacon for himself at home. He reached for his hearing aids and popped them in.

"Dr Roy! Whatever are you doing here?"

"Smelling that magnificent bacon," the Doc replied. He became aware that it was Heather the book shop lady's voice and it all came flooding back to him. He was surrounded by books of all ages and types.

"Did we lock you in? Why ever didn't you ring? You must be freezing! Where's Miss KP? Here, have this bacon roll; I'll bring you some tea."

"Someone locked us in!" Dr Roy said sheepishly. "I suppose it was my fault. I paid for my purchases, so I expect you thought we'd gone, but Eleanor was at the back of the shop, and we lost track of time. She's there now, I hope, on the sofa."

Eleanor had indeed heard voices and came pottering over with her hair half up and half down. At least her new teeth were back in, and she smiled.

"I'm so sorry, the cookery book distracted me, and we've been making use of your facilities. I do hope you don't mind."

"Come with me, dear, you must have the other bacon roll. We'll pop out for some more, have breakfast together and run you home. This will teach me to always check each part of the shop before we shut!!"

So Mark, (Heather's husband), Heather, Eleanor and the Doc had a lovely breakfast together in the middle part of the bookshop, and they then had a lift to each home. Poppet the cat was most put out that her breakfast was very late!

The Doc still hadn't found his book about the universe!!

The Swimming Session

May had arrived. The sun was shining and spring was gradually changing to summer. The weather must have been improving, as Eleanor had unstitched the red fleecy lining from her green cape.

As well as cycling, her other favourite exercise was swimming. Dr Roy was more of a walker, and occasionally would practise some yoga warm-ups in his room at home, as his grand-daughter was a yoga teacher and he had learnt a few bits and pieces from her, but he couldn't get much further than the "cat" posture and the "downward-facing dog". He wasn't keen on swimming, as it felt so cold once you came out of the pool and had to walk home or wait for a bus.

At this particular time the swimming pool had been renovated and was out of action for a few months while new changing rooms were being put in. The old communal ones were being replaced with separate cubicles, and a new "gym" (or fitness centre, as Eleanor liked to call it), had been opened upstairs.

There had always been an outdoor pool, but even on warm days it was too cold and busy for the pair of them.

"Let's go and have a swim," said Eleanor one Saturday. "It makes a change from the bookshop, or lunch. We can have a meal afterwards."

Dr Roy wasn't keen, but thought he would go as he should try to keep fit. He was eating rather too many pies and cakes these days.

So off they went by bus, through the town, towards the river, past the church with the wonky steeple. Once there, they were offered concessionary tickets by the smiley lady at the reception desk.

They got ready in the new, sparkling, turquoise changing rooms and went to put their belongings into adjacent lockers. Eleanor of course put her lorgnette in her handbag inside her large swimming bag, and put on a flowery

1970's swimming cap. Roy took a while longer, as he had to take out his special shell hearing aids and put them in their container, near the top of the bag so he could find them easily when he came out. His towel also had to be near the top, but he no longer worried about washing his hair, as he hardly had any left.

Now, of course, he couldn't hear what Eleanor was saying, so she tried to communicate with him by pointing and signing, "deep", "shallow" and showing on her fingers how many lengths of the pool she was intending to swim. This was a session for everybody today, and there were quite a few children doing headstands and jumping in off the side, as well as adults doing lengths in various strokes – one man was bombing up and down in the fast lane doing a sort of demented "butterfly" stroke, and ladies were swimming and chatting at the same time in the slow lane. Eleanor couldn't read the signs saying whether each lane was "slow" "medium" or "fast", so Dr Roy had to sign to her they needed to duck underneath the rope to go into the slow lane as they were getting in the way of an agitated young man who seemed to be doing part backstroke, part crawl and part side–stroke, wearing a headband which made him look like a bandit.

After they had done ten lengths, dodging children and supposed professionals, they spotted some steps at the side of the pool, which seemed to be going upwards. Eleanor looked at Roy, signing "bubbles" as best she could, and mouthing "Jacuzzi", thinking that was upstairs, and Dr Roy was signing to her as if drinking, and said "Maybe it's the cafe?" The stairs were very narrow, and they could only go in single file, which they each thought quite odd. At the top were a lot of children who seemed to be in a queue. Was it an ice- cream stall? They didn't seem to be coming back with anything.

"Excuse me; I do need to ask, "said a lady with "LIFE GUARD" on her yellow top, and red shorts. "Do you have any medical or heart condition?"

"Certainly not!" said Eleanor. What on earth was wrong with eating or drinking, when these children obviously were? Then, she realised, no one came back that way as they were going, one at a time, when the lady life guard gave permission, down a chute!

"Goodness me, will we end up back in the pool?" she asked, feeling foolish, as she could now see, of course, the chute wound round like a long snake over part of the pool.

"Sit up if you don't want to go too fast," advised the guard, "and I will wait for you to come out before I send the next person down".

"Roy, my dear, look are you OK with this?" she asked at the top of her voice, showing him where he would end up, in a little area cordoned off, "and you must move out of the way quickly , before the next person comes down."

Dr Roy didn't like the look of it at all, but didn't dare say he wanted to go back down the steps, as more and more children were now behind them. So Eleanor went first, after a young boy who said "Don't worry, it's great!" She lay down, forgetting the instructions, but worried she was going too fast so sat up again. After whizzing round bends and landing with a "splosh", she recovered herself and got out to wait for Roy. He had remembered to sit up, and kept his eyes tightly closed, dreaming of the Bakewell tart he was going to try to find later.

They then decided to go and get dressed, before finding the cafe, (which was indeed up a different flight of steps) where they admitted they'd had quite a shock but felt quite exhilarated!

 On the way to the cafeteria they stumbled upon a large yellow plastic trunk of a figure, with no arms, standing in the corridor. A little further on was a red one, and a blue one.

"Oh", remarked Dr Roy to Eleanor, "Don't you think they look like three characters with surnames of those colours, from a well- known detective board game?"

"They do. I wonder if you can play that game here by the side of the pool?"

"I'm afraid not," a young gentleman replied, after overhearing their conversation. "They're for practising lifesaving!"

"Of course! How silly I am."

They ordered a couple of cups of coffee, and a group of children came over to their table. "We saw you go down the chute, and we were well impressed!" said one of them.

"Didn't you go down just before us?"asked Roy of the young chap who'd told them it was great.

"Yes! Hope you enjoyed it".

"Well, it was an experience," came the reply. They each had a lovely baked potato for lunch, and laughed about their swim. Dr Roy bought a couple of Bakewell tarts from the bakery on their way home, which they enjoyed later on.

The "Out of Date" shopping list

Eleanor's friend Hermione had recently had her eighty-fifth birthday, but unfortunately felt poorly and was taken into hospital soon afterwards. Eleanor didn't live too far from the hospital and had a trusty bicycle, her "Wayfarer". It had a basket on the front in which she had a bunch of seedless grapes and a card, as well as her handbag which contained her lorgnette amongst other items.

She had a bit of trouble finding the right ward, as she'd mixed up "Mendlesham" and "Rendlesham" and almost gone into the neonatal ward. She eventually found the correct women's ward and there was Hermione in the last bed on the left, sitting up and smiling, reading a book. It was "Don Quixote".

"Goodness me, Hermione, are you reading that in Spanish or English?"

"Oh, English, of course, dear. I can't remember any Spanish now. I love these chivalrous characters, and tales of madness."

Eleanor couldn't remember where Hermione had learnt some Spanish. Had she gone to Spain in the seventies, or had she been a Spanish teacher? It was a very unusual choice of book to read in hospital. Surely it wasn't a quick or easy read?

"How are you feeling?"

"Well, I've had an awfully upset stomach and terrible arthritis in my legs, but otherwise I'm not so bad for my age. How are you, Eileen sweetie?"

"I'm Eleanor, and I'm not so bad thanks." She couldn't remember what Hermione was in hospital for, but it probably wasn't to do with her stomach or legs. She'd definitely been told to cut down on smoking recently, so maybe it was to do with that?

Hermione gratefully accepted the grapes; "I do love grapes, they're not too heavy on the stomach."

"Yes indeed," came the reply. "Is there anything else I can get you from the shops?"

"I'm fine at the moment, but before I go home I'll let you have a list, thank you."

Well, the following week when Eleanor went to visit the hospital Hermione had a list as long as her arm.

"Pearlete denture powder" was at the top of the list. Could you still buy that? Eleanor stared at the list through her lorgnette.

"Shortex pastry margarine

Pelaw bun flour

Sure Shield Fruit Laxatives

Powdered domestic borax

Semolina

Pelaw floor polish

CWS Bath cubes

Sutox beef suet

Spel Washing Powder"

Goodness me! What was going on? Shortex! Eleanor was sure her mother used to make pastry with that when she was a child. She didn't know what to say. There was a lot of hustle and bustle around them and she thought she'd best leave Hermione, and would add bread, milk and fruit to the list before taking the items round to the house.

"Are you sure you can still get these?" she tentatively asked. "I can get you some ready-made pastry if you like."

"As you wish, don't worry. They should all be in the Co-Op." She handed Eleanor two twenty pound notes – which Eleanor peered at suspiciously in case they were some pre-Decimalisation paper currency.

"Well, I'll do my best. Shall I bring them to yours once I know you're there?"

"Yes please. I'll let you know."

So, the following Thursday Eleanor heard that Hermione was home and went around, again on her bicycle, with the items on the list, or the closest, in the basket and in some panniers she sometimes attached to the back of her bicycle.

"I'm sorry, Hermione. A lot of those brands don't exist anymore. Pelaw, isn't that the Co-Op's brand from years ago? I got you another floor polish. I had to get self-raising flour, not bun flour....but do you do all that baking? And as for bath cubes......"

"Oh, Eleanor!" Hermione suddenly laughed out loud. "I'm so sorry; I gave you the wrong list! I had so many bad nights' sleep there, and had a doze in the daytime, and dreamt of all those items in a green-framed shop. Do you remember the Co-op when we were kiddies? I wrote the things from the dream all down in the morning, and then did you a shopping list, and of course gave you the wrong one. You must have thought I'd gone nuts!"

"Well, I wasn't sure if it was all part of a big act! You did love the stage."

"I did indeed. Thank you for the pastry though, when the grand–kiddies come I can make a pie. "Ariel" washing powder, that's fine," she fished out the items. "Bubble bath, don't you miss those cubes? Don't they have bath bombs these days?"

"I must say I prefer a shower, I don't like climbing in the bath nowadays," said Eleanor. "Bath bombs sound a bit modern for me! Oh, I hope you don't mind "Steradent", I don't even know if you have dentures!"

"I don't!"

This rather shocked Eleanor, as she herself had some, and felt Hermione had been neglecting her teeth.

"How about semolina? Do you need it, if you have your own teeth? Isn't it too soft? Oh, that reminds me...I didn't dare get laxatives for you. I think you're best to stick to liquorice!"

"Ha!! The grandkiddies won't eat semolina! I don't need laxatives, my dear! I see you've got me some shop-brand floor cleaner, I'm going to have the cleanest floors in the town, what with the polish!"

"How about the beef suet? I didn't get you that. If you want stew and dumplings, I'll take you to the "Snooty Fox" for some. They do a senior citizen special on a Tuesday".

"That would be splendid," beamed Hermione. "By the way I'm going to look up some old shopping lists and things. I think I still have my parents' old dividend number from the Co-op. I do miss those times, don't you?"

"I do indeed," sighed Eleanor. She never did get to the bottom of why Hermione was reading "Don Quixote" or what had been wrong with her, but the crazy shopping list was resolved.

Going out with a bang

Colonel Cedric Tomkin (Retired) was an old "flame" of Eleanor's friend Hermione. He was a tall, elegantly dressed gentleman in his late eighties, and had been a good "catch" in his youth. He had had a couple of wives, two sons and a daughter and now had several grandchildren. He and Hermione had spent a few years in each other's company in the last decade and eventually parted ways for two reasons. The first was that he had a love of speeding along quiet country lanes in his old white Ford Sierra. He fortunately didn't hit any moving objects, but he frightened her. The other reason was that he was a terrible flirt still, with a roving eye. He would wink at ladies in the street, sometimes causing his monocle to fall out. He didn't particularly need this item, but thought it was a good way of chatting up members of the opposite sex, as well as looking intelligent.

He was also a collector of driving licence points. Up until his eighties he had always got away with his whizzing along country lanes. He had excellent eyesight and reflexes in the old days. However on this particular occasion a letter dropped onto his doormat one morning stating he had been caught in the village of "Little Piffling" going at thirty-six miles an hour in a thirty mile an hour area. This would mean three points on his licence. He didn't even recollect going there, and had to rule out a couple of lady friends before he could decide whether to contest the points. He had recently been out with Ethel, who lived in the same block of warden–controlled flats. She had got upset with him patting her behind with his walking stick when they arrived at their destination, which he couldn't remember. Was it the teashop? The misdemeanour could have been the day he'd taken Sophia out. She had been keener on him than he on her, but he wanted to let her down gently and had not yet managed to do so. She was too "clingy" and not adventurous enough for him.

He phoned Ethel first.

"Hello, gorgeous". He knew this would irritate her. "Cedric here. Do you remember when we went to the matinee of the "Trousermap"? Did we go through a village called Little Piffling?"He tended to get words mixed up if he was a bit nervous.

"I think you mean the "Mousetrap", came the curt reply."I've never been to the theatre with you, and I never will. I don't want you telephoning me again." With that, she flung the 'phone down.

He tried Sophia next, knowing she wouldn't be so rude. He didn't really want to speak to her, but of course, she was delighted to hear his military tones on the other end of the 'phone.

"Of course I remember Piffling. Didn't we laugh at the name?" It may not have been the truth, but she certainly made out that it was. "What a marvellous day we had!"

"Well, I've got a speeding ticket. Points on my licence and all that."

"I'm so sorry", she said in cloying tones. "I do remember now, didn't we see a sort of tall horse box in a lay–by? I remember asking you if you thought it was to transport alpacas. We wondered if we saw ears sticking out of the top. Well, I reckon there was a speed gun in there, and it's illegal as it should be visible. I should argue about it if I were you. But I'll help you towards any fine."

"Not to worry. Can't be helped. Toodlepip for now." He was now talking in his usual military-style clipped tones. He was used to barking orders from his army days.

He sat and contemplated the situation. What did it matter to have points on his licence, now he was eighty-seven? He surely wouldn't be driving once he was ninety; did it matter if the points were on his licence for three years? Of course not! Maybe he could even collect a few more.

Well, he sent off his licence and paid the fine. He decided he couldn't be bothered to mention the alpaca-transporting box and whether it was legal because Sophia may have been making it all up just so that she could see him again.

A few months later when the weather improved he and a few of his friends were invited to a "bash" for Ray and Mildred's sixtieth wedding anniversary. Ray had been his friend for many years, and they lived in the same town. This was to be held in a sort of bistro cafe, which became a private venue in the evening, in a nearby seaside town.

A few people from Cedric's block of flats were invited; there was Les, who had an assistance dog called Hades, and Doreen, a rather bony lady. Another couple of friends from the town wanted to go, and there weren't really enough drivers. Cedric actually needed to fit six people in the car plus himself and the dog, who was quite a large husky.

Cedric had been involved in the peace-keeping force in Cyprus in the 1950s and had jumped out of more planes than he could shake a stick at. He had kept some of the parachute straps in case they came in useful some time, and was now able to make bigger belts by adding extensions like those for pregnant ladies, so he could fit an extra person in both the front and back, as long as he or she were slim.

The evening in question soon arrived. The party started at six thirty, and he had to collect Eleanor and Dr Roy, neither of whom was well known to him. They lived on the other side of town. There was Bessie Barker to collect on the way, and her brother Cuthbert, who had known Cedric since his school-days. Ray and Mildred had asked if he would kindly collect these people.

It was quite a squeeze in the car, as the slimmer ones were two in the front seat with an extendable belt (Cuthbert and Les), and two slimmer ones sharing an extendable belt in the back (Doreen and Eleanor). Dr Roy and Bessie had a "proper" seat to themselves as they were a little more portly. Various gifts, including pot plants and bottles of wine, picture frames and chocolates, as well as all the ladies' handbags, the Colonel's collapsible walking stick and Cuthbert's walking frame were all in the boot, as well as a bowl and food for Hades. The dog himself was in the back footwell, sometimes near Dr Roy and sometimes near Eleanor, sniffing her as she smelt of cat.

A wonderful time was had by all, and the same ladies and gents got back in the same seats for the return journey. However, they hadn't got very far along the main "A" road when a police car seemed to be flashing a light at them with "STOP" in its windscreen, and it was making an odd sound, not quite a siren, but similar.

"Drat and Fiddlesticks" muttered the colonel, deciding to stop in the next lay by. He pulled in and looked in the rear view mirror. A portly police officer, Sergeant Hopper, jumped out of the four by four and rushed up to Cedric's now open window.

"'Ello, 'ello! What's going on 'ere then? Your suspension looks dodgy; the car's almost on the ground." He peered into the back of the car.

"Four in the back, eh?"

"Er – five, actually," ventured Eleanor, who was too honest for her own good.

"Five?"He peered into the footwell, expecting a child or worse? another elderly person? There, lifting his head and yawning, was Hades, his tail wrapped around Doreen and Eleanor on the near side, and his front paws round Dr Roy and Bessie.

"Aren't you a bit ambitious, Sir?" Hopper addressed the colonel.

"Ambitious is a word many have used to describe me," retorted the latter. "If you are referring to the number of people, fortunately my companions are skinny."

"And what is the seatbelt situation here, Sir?"

"Well," began Cedric. "I'm a retired Colonel from the parachute regiment, and I've made extra belts from parachute straps. I can assure you they are quite safe. As you can see, I survived every jump."

"I don't care if you're a colonel or the King of England, these straps are NOT safe," snapped Hopper. "You're breaking the law!" He puffed himself up as large as he could, going as red as a beetroot and almost bursting the top buttons of his jacket.

"Steady on," Eleanor piped up. "This gentleman's doing us all a favour. And we ARE octogenarians!"

"I don't care if you're Octogenarians, Vegetarians, Rastafarians, Veterinarians or Antidisestablishmentarians! You're breaking the law!"

"Well," muttered Doreen. "I wouldn't say I was a Rastafarian, although I do like Bob Marley."

"You've got an awful lot of long words there. Maybe you should be on "Call My Bluff?!" Bessie suggested. What's more, can you spell them?"

"Gracious me, is that what he called you? Rastafarian?" asked Dr Roy, who had missed most of the conversation as one hearing aid had slipped.

Sergeant Hopper looked to the back at Roy, saw a bit of shell poking out of his ear, and laughed. He started off by quietly tittering, and then the noise got louder, gradually became guffaws, and then hoots. He held on to the car – one hand on the door handle and the other on the open window frame for support, and almost split his sides laughing. His top button popped right off.

"I'm glad we cheered up your evening," volunteered the colonel, solemnly, his monocle popping out again. "I'd offer you a seat, but I can't fit you in."

"I'm so sorry," Hopper dried his eyes. He tried not to laugh, but ended up snorting instead. "You've made my day. I've met some right hooligans and nasty pieces of work today, but you seven have really made me laugh. I'm sorry I have to report the driver for over–loading the car, but I promise I'll make it up to you."

"Make it up? Indeed? I'd like to see that. You'd better not ban me, or we'll be stuck." The colonel was not impressed.

"Introduce me to everyone, and then I'll take your details."

"This is Doreen, otherwise known as "Soreen". You can guess why. Les, and his helping dog Hades," He gestured towards them." Dr Roy Burrows and his friend Eleanor Kyson–Pointer, and Bessie Barker and Cuthbert Sharpe, brother and sister. I'm Cedric Tomkin, you know all about me. Yes, I have three points on my licence, and will probably have another few now. Never mind, I'm almost eighty-eight." He gave his address, and they moved on, dropping everyone safely home.

A few weeks later an envelope dropped onto Cedric's doormat- this time another three points to go on his licence, for over–loading the vehicle. He had only just got his licence back from the first three, but sent it back. Sergeant Hopper had described him as "being of good character" so he was still allowed to drive.

Some months later, yet another brown envelope made its way to the colonel. It was asking for his insurance to be renewed. He had had his eyes tested at Speccles(the optician) and was pronounced fit to drive, so he put the renewal letter on the back of the sofa intending to sort it out in a few days' time. He by now had another lady friend by the name of Charlotte, with whom he was getting on famously well. They often had a cuddle of an evening on the sofa.

Imagine Cedric's horror when, just before Christmas, another envelope, this time with a demand in red lettering, for the insurance money. He couldn't believe he hadn't paid it, until he came to vacuuming behind the sofa, and there was the original demand. He took it to the Post Office together with a few other bills he intended to pay at once, his electricity and others, but alas, it ended up at the bottom of the pile amongst his library books, and it never made it to the cashier's till.

By now the retired colonel was so taken up with his new lady friend that he didn't realise there were a few things wrong with the car. One tyre was almost bald, and the left indicator wasn't flashing as it should. Now, there are very few policemen in Suffolk, but one chanced to be following him on his way from dropping Charlotte home one afternoon. He was also driving in a rather higgledy piggledy manner as he was trying to tune the radio to catch an interesting talk on the hobbies of retired army personnel.

Sure enough, the policeman flashed him a few times and signalled to him to pull in, which he did.

"Excuse me, Sir, you're wavering," said the constable, a middle-aged, balding man with a dour expression. "Did you know your left indicator isn't working, and one tyre is almost bald? I'd like to see your insurance documents, please."

"I didn't know, old chap. I'll bring the documents in when I can, to the station," the

Colonel offered."I was wavering as I'm trying to locate Radio Suffolk".

Of course, when he came to look for the papers, he couldn't find them. He was sure he'd sorted that insurance, but when he checked his bank statement the transaction wasn't there.

"Oh no, I think I've had it now. No more driving for me!"That was now twelve points on his licence, as driving without insurance was another six points.

He got in touch with Sergeant Hopper, and explained the situation. His new–found friend thought he probably had a case to avoid having more points, as he genuinely believed he had sorted the insurance and after all he was eighty –eight, but did he really want to drive? He had a bus pass, and his sons and daughter would help out if necessary.

His grandson Daniel had just passed his driving test aged twenty, and the family were organising a party to celebrate. Cedric decided he would do up the Sierra and present it to

Daniel. In the meantime Sergeant Hopper stuck to his word...and helped out on little excursions in his time off, taking the group on little day trips and soirees, sometimes even borrowing the police minibus and wearing his police helmet and driving gloves. Occasionally he took his wife Linda on the little jaunts, and she became friendly with the ladies.

Cedric's driving licence (the paper part) was returned with "DISQUALIFIED" written diagonally across it, and Hopper had it framed to be presented at the same family gathering at which Cedric handed the car keys to his grandson.

Everyone roared with laughter as Cedric received the framed licence from his son Julian. His monocle popped out as he took a sip of champagne, just as Daniel announced:

"Well you could call it going out with a bang, though not a literal one!" and the family cheered.

"It was just one of those days"

Dr Roy had given up driving some time ago partly because he had a bus pass, and partly because of his hearing. His brother Dean would transport him in his old "Fiesta" if he needed to be anywhere very important or off the beaten track. His friend Eleanor had a bicycle, which she'd had for many years, but if they went anywhere very local together they went by feet.

It was Eleanor's birthday, and Dr Roy wanted to take her to a lovely little farm cafe for a special lunch. He asked Dean if he was free to drive, which he was, and he asked Eleanor to wear her best clothes.

"Farm cafe lunch is on me," he announced.

So she put on her new skirt and top and even wore her navy blue raincoat from her working days to make a change from her cape.

She was collected at half past ten in the old Fiesta, which rattled and groaned along in third gear. If Dean tried to go into fourth gear, it made the most dreadful noises, so he stayed in third. They were going down a country lane away from the town they all lived in, and suddenly what should be ahead of them but a huge herd of cows, being followed by a stout elderly farmer-looking gentleman in an overall and corduroys. The cattle took up the whole road, so Dean had to go down into an even lower gear, and he was getting rather agitated as he wanted his dinner. He beeped the horn at the farmer-chap, who waved benevolently and smiled, ambling on slowly. They seemed to be crawling along very slowly for what seemed like an age, but must have been half an hour. In the end Dean decided to do a three-point turn and go back the way they'd come, and try what he thought was another route. However, this was in a part of town he didn't know well, and no sooner had they turned into a very narrow road than they were greeted by lots of hooting and people winding down car windows shouting

"OY! One way street!"

"Get off the road, you nutcase!" yelled one irate bald gentleman in dark glasses.

"Keep your hair on!" Dean muttered. "Not that you've got any," he muttered under his breath.

"Oh dear," murmured Eleanor. "I think you'd best go back the other way."

"I know you two don't approve," said Dean, "But I'll have to use the sat-nav."

He pulled up on the side of the road and typed in the name of the garden centre "The Trowel and Trellis". The lady's voice then sent them a very funny old route none of them had ever travelled along before, up and down winding lanes until they came to a gentleman on the side of the road in charge of a large "STOP" sign. He seemed to be eating his lunch, or brunch, in the form of a hunk of bread and when he finally swallowed the last mouthful he turned the sign to "GO.", having received a signal from his colleague up the road with the sign for drivers coming the other way. However a few hundred yards along was a large yellow sign "DO NOT FOLLOW SATNAV", as road works were blocking the most common route.

"Oh, I'm so sorry Eleanor, your birthday seems to be turning into a fiasco!" Doctor Roy was getting quite upset now.

"Don't worry. As long as the car doesn't break down, I'm seeing some countryside and that chap with the sign did make me laugh. What a fun job, changing a sign from "Stop" to "Go!""

Dean got out of the car and asked a couple who seemed to know where they were going, and they soon had our three travellers at their destination, although by now it was mid-day.

"Would you like to eat first or look around?" Dr Roy asked Eleanor.

"Let's have a little look around. I need some bedding plants for my outdoor tubs and a mat to kneel on."

So they found these items which the two gentlemen bought for Miss Kyson-Pointer as a birthday gift, and she finally got her birthday lunch, a sort of chowder type of dish first and when her cake was delivered to the table it had a candle on top, and as well as the two chaps and staff, the customers at all the tables joined in singing "Happy birthday" to our heroine. She beamed around and blushed bright red, and thanked everyone most profusely.

However on their return to the car around three o'clock, there was a bright red flashy car parked extremely close to Dean's car.

"I'll stand behind and guide you out," offered Roy.

Alas, Dean had his foot on the wrong pedal, revved up the poor little car, and shot forwards instead of backwards. The front of the car bashed the low fence in front, and both of its passengers were rather shaken. Poor Roy, who was still behind the car, put his hands to his head in despair.

Dean managed to stop the car and get out, to inspect the fence. That was dented, as well as the front of the car being rather bashed. Luckily, the red car was not touched. He went inside to confess to the staff, but they felt sorry for him and said the fence could be sorted and not to worry. However one of them came to reverse his car out and get the trio back on their way home. That was another challenge, with all the roadworks, one way streets, and so forth, but they went via the original road with the cattle, which were fortunately by now safely in the correct field.

When they dropped Eleanor, Dr Roy said "I'm so sorry you've had a funny old birthday,"

"I suppose it was just one of those days", was the reply.

The Best Laid Plans

Eleanor was getting ready for her little break away with Dr Roy, where they were hoping to meet his best friend from his university days. She wanted to have a whole new hairstyle: perhaps a gentle blonde rather than pink tinges, and a cut so she didn't have to twirl her hair into a bun and then stick pins into it each day. Sometimes the aubergine streaks looked "purple" and Dr Roy would tease her, and he would call her "Pincushion" if she had pins in it. "I'll ask someone to recommend a hairdresser," she thought as she looked in the mirror. "I can't go away with it like this."

Well, Hermione's daughter Jeanette used a hairdresser called "Snippets" in the centre of town. She had been seeing a lady called Peggy, who unfortunately wasn't available the week Eleanor needed her hair doing. She booked instead with a lady called "Tan", presumably short for "Tanya", and sat in the chair beaming in the mirror. She was surrounded by three or four ladies all with a similar "bouffon" of rigid lacquered hair, and she wondered if all customers had this hair-do and she was causing trouble having something different.

"Would you like to take your cape off, and put on our black one?"Tan had a London accent. Eleanor took her green cape off, gave it to "Tan" to hang up, and was assisted into a silky black hairdresser's cape. "Any idea what colour or length you'd like?"

"I'd quite like to be blonder, but not too unnatural, and take a few inches off, please. I don't want to keep putting it up."

Well, after choosing from a selection of blonde colours from funny little samples of hair attached to card she sat for ages with foils in, making her look like an alien. Dr Roy went past the hairdresser on his way to the greengrocer, peering in, and couldn't recognise her. On the way back he went in and asked for her. They showed him where she was, in the window. He thought she had pieces of "Bacofoil" wrapped round sections of her hair, and they were all sticking out almost half a foot in width. She looked like nothing on earth.

"Are you taking off soon?" asked Roy. "I thought you had propellers."

"Well, I hope they will be taken off soon," replied Eleanor, who by now had finished two cups of tea and read two copies of "Woman's Weekly" and one "People's Friend". Dr Roy beat a hasty retreat as a young lady came up to remove the foils and wash Eleanor's hair. It took some time to remove them all, and the young lady talked non-stop about her husband's brother's affair with a traffic warden, and how he was let off all sorts of fines. Then it was her trip to Ibiza with her best friend from school who fell out with the hotel manager and they all had to change hotel. Her clothing (shorts and skimpy top) was as scanty as her chatter was excessive. After she had rinsed Eleanor's hair at the basin she was escorted back to the styling chair to see the colour of her hair.....AAGH! EEEEK! The young lady disappeared mysteriously, and Tan cautiously returned.

"Oh, my Goodness!" shrieked Eleanor. "It's MUSTARD colour!!"

"It wasn't meant to turn out QUITE that colour!" said Tanya. "I'm so sorry, maybe I left it too long. Are you not happy? I think it suits you."

"I look like the scarecrow from a children's programme years ago!!"

"Well, I'll trim it for you, and if you wash it in a day or two it will settle."

Tanya cut a few inches off Eleanor's rather mustard-coloured mop.

"I have an outing with a friend on Monday," wailed Eleanor. "I will have to wear a hat now!"

"It will be fine by then," Tan tried to reassure her. "I won't charge you if you aren't happy."

Her hair was now a sort of bob, and far too modern for her. She wasn't sure whether she liked it.

"Hair always grows back," Tan's positive voice chirped on. "The colour will grow out before you know it. I'll pop you under the dryer for a while, and then would you like me to use the straighteners?"

"I most certainly would not!" shouted Eleanor, quite irate by now. "I'll sit under the dryer, but I have lived all these years without straightening my hair. How ridiculous! Perms for straight hair are one thing, but who would want to make non–curly hair straight?"

"Everyone likes the straighteners," Tan said very quietly.

"Well I'm NOT everyone!!"

So she sat under an old-style dryer (which was the only part of the experience she enjoyed), but got involved with reading some cookery articles, as well as some on the royal family's misdemeanours, and Tanya forgot her as she was busy with various young ladies. When the dryer was finally taken off, her hair had gone bone–dry and straw–like, and what with the mustard colour, she really did resemble that scarecrow–like character. Fortunately, "Snippets" didn't charge anything, and offered another free appointment in six weeks, but Eleanor decided she couldn't face the place again.

Dr Roy had arranged for Dean to collect her when she'd finished. She went to the car park they'd parked in earlier, and she thought she'd found the right blue "Fiesta". However, on opening the back door on the passenger side, she was greeted with a stony "I think you've got the wrong car, madam!" from a lady with a walking-stick.

"I'm awfully sorry," Eleanor remarked. She walked round the back of the car. The lady then opened her window and seeing Eleanor at the next car, also a blue "Fiesta", said "Look at the registration!" and Eleanor realised with horror that someone else in the town had an equally ancient car that probably didn't go above third gear!

Dr Roy, who was already back at the car, said her hair looked nice, and called her "The Blonde Bombshell" instead of "Pincushion" but for a few days she wore a large pink floppy hat over it until they went away. Her friend Hermione did say she should maybe see Peggy next time, and Eleanor agreed to think about it.

Fifty Shades of Purple

Eleanor gingerly opened her wardrobe door. It was time to pack some clothes for her few days away in the Dales, where she was going with Dr Roy to meet one of his old University friends. She seemed to be seeing each item with a new pair of eyes. Ninety per cent of the clothes had been bought at least thirty years ago. There were long skirts, some from the seventies, all beige or faded blue with flowers, swirls or Paisley print, all a sad version of their former colours. Next she spotted some Polo-necked jumpers, also from the seventies, in black, navy blue, and possibly a cream colour, all looking moth-eaten now. She came across a few pairs of trousers she had worn years ago, when she used to be a secretary to a professor, but which she hadn't dared wear recently, and some blouses which had "Lady Di" frilly necklines and some which tied up with bows. She looked with horror at all of these.

"I can't go away with any of these!" she muttered to herself. "They all look as though they've come from a car boot sale. I can't believe I haven't bought any new items other than hats, scarves and underwear since my working days, at the turn of the century. It's time to get some cash from the bank and take myself to a clothes shop."

As a lady who didn't like change, or modern items, she detested bank cards, so decided to take out a wad of cash from her new bank, at the cashier's desk.

"Ooh, are you doing something special?" the young lady with perfectly long gelled nails asked, as she handed over the cash.

"Well, actually, yes. I need some new clothes for going away."

The lady looked at Eleanor's cape, and wondered whether she would take that.

"Enjoy yourself then, darlin'," she said.

Eleanor walked down to a boutique she hadn't been in before.

"Lovely day, isn't it?" a bright middle-aged lady with curly hair greeted her as she entered. "I'm Sue."

"Indeed it is," Eleanor swept in and closed the door.

"Are you looking for something special?" Sue asked.

"Well, I am, actually. I haven't bought any new clothes in years. I need everything from tops, bottoms, cardigans; the lot. I'm more or less starting from scratch."

"Well, you have a good figure," the lady bounced over and studied Eleanor's slim shape as she took off her cape."What's your favourite colour?"

"Ooh, I've never really thought about that." It was true, Eleanor hadn't had a favourite colour since she was a schoolgirl. In those days, she'd loved red. But she could hardly go on a train trip as an octogenarian, with a gentleman of a similar age, in red. It would be almost as embarrassing as wearing her old clothes.

Admittedly the lining of her cape, which she put in during the winter, was red, but you couldn't see that most of the time.

She thought to herself, well I'm not keen on blue, or pink. What colour was that lady in the bank wearing on her nails? They certainly hadn't been her own nails. They had looked quite unnatural, long and pointy, like those of a witch, but what colour had they been? Not lilac, delicate or subtle, but a deep purple. It had actually been a very striking colour.

"Purple! Maybe I'll try purple!" she exclaimed suddenly. The curly-haired lady had been pointing at various items while Eleanor was thinking. They were all sort of beige and flowery, rather like her previous clothes in fact, but a slightly more modern version of everything. The more she saw those garments, beige blouses with flowers, and pastel blue skirts with spots and stripes, the more she decided she was going to have a whole new wardrobe based on purple. Sue looked at her for a moment, and then went off to find a long mauve skirt elegantly shaped in panels, and a shirt with a collar, pale lilac, simple but stylish, and held them against Eleanor.

"Yes, I like it. It suits you, this colour. Would you like to try them on?"

"Ooh yes. Can I take a whole assortment of clothes into the changing room please?"

"Of course. Are you a size ten?"

Indeed Eleanor was around that size, as she had lost some weight in recent years. For the next couple of hours she tried various outfits on, with more and more items being found, and brought over including a dress, purple tights, as well as skirts, tops and cardigans. At one stage Sue came over with a whole pile of scarves, lovely and silky. One was beige with purple horse patterns, there was a deep purple one with yellow spots, a lilac one with a lovely crinkly texture, a fluffy one and another one which was a sort of "seaweed" texture, like purple tails.

"Do any of these take your fancy?"

Eleanor looked at all of them. Each one went with one outfit or another, so she decided to be extravagant and take all of them. As she was about to pay she passed some little lightweight rain jackets.

"Ooh - my cape isn't really waterproof," she pondered. "I think I'll need a raincoat too." There was a lovely lilac one with little purple umbrellas on it. That went into the lavender-coloured bag full of purchases. She thanked Sue for her help, after paying – there was just enough money in the large wad of cash - and even popped to the bank to thank the lady with the purple nails, who was quite flattered to have inspired a whole new wardrobe.

Once home she 'phoned Dr Roy to tell him of her new purchases.

"Fifty shades of purple, eh?" he joked. "The Yorkshire Dales people won't know what's hit them!"

"Mistaken Identity"

Dr Roy had a friend called Leslie Hawkins with whom he'd been to University, almost seventy years ago. He'd kept in touch with him for the first fifteen years or so, and they'd attended one another's weddings, and children's christenings, and so on, but they'd lost touch since their children had grown up. They had studied philosophy together, and Leslie had gone on to teach, whereas the Doc had done some research work, got his PhD and then other bits and pieces of different types of work.

"I do miss dear old Leslie. I wonder if he's still alive," sighed Roy as he was visiting his son Jake one day. "I think he last lived somewhere in Scotland, but I'm not sure where he'd be now."

His daughter-in-law Jennifer suggested looking on "google" ("If he was a teacher in a good school he's probably mentioned there.")

They spent some time poring over the computer together, and eventually came across a few people of that name, but they were all in America or clearly not the Leslie Dr Roy was looking for.

He spent the next few weeks searching the flat for old address books. He eventually found one from the late 1960's, and there under "H" was a number for Leslie Hawkins.

The Doctor was quite excited, and decided to try and ring that very evening.

A very distant–sounding Scottish voice answered:-

"Hullo there! What can I do you for, wee laddie?"

"Hallo, old chap! Is that you, Leslie? Your old friend Roy here, from many moons ago; how the Devil are you?"

The voice at the other end was indeed in Scotland, and didn't have the greatest hearing. The gentleman wasn't sure if he had a friend called Roy or not, but his wife was convinced that he had, in fact, had a friend Roy many years ago. "Ask him if he remembers The Power Ballroom, where we used to go every Saturday evening," she urged him.

"I do remember the Tower Ballroom," Roy bellowed down the telephone, as that was where he had met his wife Sandra, who had unfortunately died in the last ten years. "Shall we meet up? I say, send me an e-mail, and we'll arrange it that way. My hearing isn't that great, even with my new hearing aids."

So he gave his e-mail address to the gentleman and a few days later a message arrived. It seemed very odd that the address didn't contain Leslie's name or surname, but never mind, e-mail addresses were a bit modern for him; he would have to ask Jennifer to help him.

"Dear Roy

It was marvellous to speak to you the other day after so many years.

Can you make Thursday April 20th or27th or one of the last two Thursdays in May? Where are you living these days? We are in

Edinburgh, where would be half way? We are both looking forward to seeing you,

Love W and D".

Roy was a bit surprised at the "W" but thought maybe it was a funny "L", and at the "D" as he thought Leslie's wife was Michelle, but maybe he was with someone else now...Where on earth would be half way between Beccles and Edinburgh?

They had another look on "Google". Knaresborough, near Harrogate, seemed to be a half way point for them to meet up. Surely though, they would have to go on a little holiday. They couldn't go for a day! He'd like to take Eleanor with him.

"Hello L and D

I think we'd best make a little holiday out of it. I'll bring my good friend Eleanor as sadly my wife left the earth a few years ago. How about Harrogate? May would be better I think.

All the best,

Roy".

Well, this seemed a good idea, and the two pairs of people booked different methods of transport, but arranged to meet in the same small hotel, the "Dales Delight" for a meal on the day after arriving. Eleanor and Dr Roy would be staying there, but the other couple were going to stay with a relative on the other side of Harrogate. Eleanor was quite excited as she hadn't been away for quite a few years, as she used to go with Hermione before she became nervous of travelling. She and Dr Roy were to get a train up there and the other couple got a coach down. Eleanor had her new assortment of purple clothes, including a rain coat, and had bought a pair of low-heeled smart black shoes. She still took her cape in case it was a bit "nippy" up north, and because the cape had served her well for so many years.

Dr Roy's brother Dean was taking them to the station, and Bessie, one of their friends who was an animal lover, was going to look after Poppet the cat for Eleanor.

The sun shone brightly on a Monday morning in mid-May. They arrived at the station amongst a bit of splendour and finery. The mayor was opening a new platform, and lots of people in posh clothes were strutting around. Someone thought Eleanor, in her new purple outfit with cardigan and tights, was a celebrity! Her hair had been coloured, as you may remember, but had now calmed down into a gentle blonde, and was also in a neat "bob" rather than her previous bun with pins sticking out.

"Could I have your autograph, please?" asked a middle-aged gentleman reaching out towards her.

"I'm not well-known, I'm afraid," replied Eleanor, dashing after Dr Roy who seemed to know which platform they were heading for.

"Was that gentleman calling me your shorter half?" asked the Doctor as they sat on a bench waiting for the train. "I know you are taller than me in those black shoes." Indeed Eleanor was already a couple of inches taller than he was.

"No," she laughed. "He asked for my autograph." They were still laughing at this when they were in their seats, in the quiet coach, and several businessmen gave them cross looks.

"I wonder who he mistook you for?"

"Well, with this bob hair-do, I wonder if I look a bit like a famous mature lady chef?" Eleanor was a huge fan of the famous cake-maker.

"You do, actually," a lady a bit further down from them joined in, and it was discussed for at least the first half hour of the journey. She and Dr Roy then settled down to a game of cards. At one stage, an elderly gentleman deposited a cup of tea in front of Eleanor, and when she asked if it was for her, he apologetically said "I'm so sorry, I thought you were my wife!"

The second leg of the train journey was also quite fun, as Eleanor wondered why the guard was carrying a table tennis bat, and holding it up.

"Are you all having a game of ping-pong once the train has gone?" she asked.

"I wish!"he retorted. "Got nine more hours to work!"

After three train changes and some rather dried–up sandwiches, and railway tea, they arrived exhausted at Harrogate station. It was still daylight, but they hailed a taxi from the station to the "Dales Delight". It had been a long day, so they unpacked their bags after a lovely cup of tea and a scone with the host and hostess.

"You're up to see an old friend, aren't you?" asked Mrs Proctor, the landlady.

"That's right," Roy answered. "Met him at Uni, in nineteen fifty-three."

"I understand you meet him tomorrow. I hope you'll recognise him after all this time!"

"That's right. He and his lady are staying with relatives. I have no idea how he looks now!"

Eleanor and Dr Roy had a light evening meal and retired to their rooms, deciding to meet for breakfast at nine the next morning.

Tuesday morning, alas, began with pouring rain, relentlessly lashing the windows.

"Thank Goodness Leslie and his lady are coming here," said Dr Roy over breakfast, which happened to be kippers and lovely oatcakes. They then got chatting to a few other guests and almost forgot they were meant to meet Leslie and his wife at half past twelve.

It was almost 12.45 when a bedraggled couple of people arrived under an inside-out umbrella which they put down into a waste–paper basket at the front door of the hotel. Firstly in stepped a gentleman perhaps about sixty with a balding head and wearing soaked jeans and a now ruined Van Heusen shirt. The lady looked younger, with a long "hippie" style skirt and little ankle boots, and her long hair would have been lovely but was soaked and stuck to her head.

Mr Proctor was nearby and offered the couple some towels and slippers so they could take off their shoes.

"Are you here to meet Eleanor and Roy?"he asked them.

"Who?" The gentleman seemed a bit deaf. "I'm here to meet my friend Roy, indeed". He certainly spoke with a Scottish accent, so was hopefully the gentleman they were meeting.

"I'll take you over to them; they're chatting to guests in the lounge."

The dishevelled couple followed the host to the lounge, where four or five people were laughing and drinking coffee. Dr Roy immediately looked at the clock and thought, Golly Gosh, is this Leslie and his lady? He got up with an outstretched hand.

"I'm Roy Burrows, and I hope you're Leslie Hawkins. I have to say, you look young! And this is...?" he gestured to the lady, who was vigorously drying her hair with a towel.

"This is my second wife Deanne, and I am Wesley, not Leslie. I thought you were my friend Roy from the office, at Higgins' place, and we used to go dancing every Saturday at the "Power Ballroom", in Blackpool, with you and your wife."

Well, this was all getting a bit complicated for Dr Roy, who was by now quite embarrassed.

He had the wrong person altogether! He had gone dancing in a posh hall called the "Tower Ballroom", all those years ago, but surely it was in Saint Andrews..? Eleanor came over to be introduced, and he had to say that the gentleman was in fact not Leslie the teacher but Wesley, who when asked about his work nudged and winked, refusing to explain what went on at "Higgins'".

"Never mind," said Eleanor. "We can all have another coffee, and get to know you both anyway. Aren't we meant to be having lunch?"

They went into the dining room and ordered some hot meals, two of fish and two of chicken.

"Ooh, there's a set of those three-sided dominoes," Deanne spotted a game in a pile on the sideboard, and brought it over. So the two couples got to know one another quite well over this game and a few others they found. They learnt all about Roy, Wesley and Deanne's marriages and children, and all about the real Leslie Hawkins too, or what was remembered of him. It was discovered that they all enjoyed watching plays, and would see one during the week. The stories about Eleanor and Roy's group of friends and their experiences were also recounted. Wesley and Deanne laughed their heads off at the tales of the Colonel and his driving licence, the swimming pool chute, being locked overnight in a second-hand bookshop, and at Eleanor's experience at the optician. She had to use her lorgnette to see the numbers on the triangular dominoes, and Deanne was fascinated by it.

"Fancy them making you one of those, these days!" she exclaimed. "You *were* lucky!"

"Yes, I'm ever so pleased."

The four of them were still sitting there at half past six, and the rain had almost stopped. Mr Proctor came over to see if they'd like sandwiches, but Wesley and Deanne said they'd best be getting back to Deanne's niece and her family's house. "We'll meet again tomorrow, maybe at the *Herring and Hippo* in town?" suggested Wesley. Mr Proctor said he would draw them a map so they could find it, and they parted company for the time being.

It was no longer pouring the next day, and they were able to sit outside at the "Herring and Hippo". A trip to the local theatre to see a comedy was booked for the last night away. The four of them had such a lovely week that they decided to meet later in the year, when Wesley and Deanne would travel to Suffolk.

The return train journey brought no problems at all, and would you believe what Dr Roy found on his door-mat when he arrived home? It was indeed a letter informing him of the funeral of his friend Leslie Hawkins! It had unfortunately been forwarded from his previous two addresses, and it was now too late for him to attend. He did however send a letter of commiseration to Leslie's wife Michelle and donated some of his savings to an equine charity as requested by Leslie.

The Speed-Dating session

There was a huge sign up on the notice board outside the main supermarket in town. "SPEED DATING FOR SENIOR CITIZENS" it read. It stated a time and place, September 5th at the Quaker Hall, at 7pm. It cost eight pounds per person, with drinks and nibbles included.

Eleanor had seen the sign each time she went shopping and wondered "Maybe I should try that. I may meet a nice gentleman. She didn't want Dr Roy to know, of course. He would consider himself to be her gentleman friend. In truth, she wanted someone she could go for bicycle rides with, maybe even on her tandem. This had been kept in her shed for many years and not been used.

Bessie Barker was going but she didn't want her brother Cuthbert to know she was looking for a gentleman. She had never been married, and was still harbouring a hope at the grand old age of seventy -nine. She ensured he was going to go to the "Snooty Fox" to play snooker with a gang of gentlemen that evening.

Colonel Tomkin was getting rather fed up with Charlotte, who was always complaining about her aches and pains, although he had very bad arthritis himself, and was now walking with two sticks. He decided to go along to see if he could find an adventurous sort of lady.

Doreen, otherwise known as "Soreen", thought she'd go along just to see what sort of people were there. Her husband had died many years ago, and she didn't know many people in the area. She had moved in the last few years to Suffolk to be near her son.

Les was also going of course, with his trusted canine companion Hades, who escorted him everywhere. He helped him around the house by loading and unloading the washing machine, retrieving dropped items, and was also able to bring emergency medication and/or the telephone should Les require these.

Well, the evening began and each person helped him or herself to a drink and plate of nibbles. The ladies all sat at separate tables, and the men had to circulate. There was roughly the same number of each; that was around twelve. Each gentleman had around three minutes to talk to each lady and then a bell would ring and he had to move on. The lady running it, who used to run the Girl Guides, now wearing "country casuals", couldn't locate her bell so decided to blow a whistle. Everyone was given a piece of paper to tick whether or not they would like to be considered as a match. Each lady had a number, and each gent a letter, so if lady 5 wanted to be considered as a match for gents E and M she would tick those letters on her form, for example. There was some very quiet jazzy music playing in the background. Was this meant to be conducive to romance?

Eleanor sat at her table, peering at her form with "A" on it through her lorgnette. A farming type of gent arrived at her table. He was very red-faced but sad-looking. Eleanor's main hobbies were cycling and baking. She told him this.

"Would I be able to ride a tandem with you?" she asked.

"Pardon?" The gentleman touched his ear and leaned forward. "You spied a phantom with me?" His wife had only died a couple of months ago and he was terrified that her ghost was there with him in the room. He gulped down his glass of non-alcoholic punch, put his paper down and fled from the Quaker Hall immediately.

Eleanor decided she'd best ask a different question next time. She asked the next chap whether he played a musical instrument. He said he could only play the comb and paper, and proceeded to do so. She could not wait for the whistle to be blown! There was the most awful noise around her, whistling hearing aids and the awful sound of the comb, together with some very sad jazz music.

In the meantime Les approached a lady in a long dark gown. She looked extremely serious.

"How long has your dog been with you?" she asked. She wasn't hugely keen on dogs.

"If you are my companion, you must accept Hades," was the answer. The lady looked horrified.

"What? You mean I have to go to the underworld?"She wondered if he was some sort of Devil-worshipper, but didn't dare say so until the last moment. He then heard "Breville" instead of "Devil", as the bell was found by the "Girl Guide leader" and sounded loudly in the background, and thought she was trying to sell him a toasted sandwich-making machine.

In the meantime Colonel Tomkin recognised Doreen from when he'd taken her to the party in his latter driving days. He thought he'd start by asking her if she liked pickling onions, just for fun, but she thought he was being a little risqué, asking if she liked tickling bunions, especially as her friend Bessie's caused her such trouble. She made it clear she wasn't interested and told him about her school-days. He then asked her "What's your tipple?"

She thought he had said "Watch your nipple!" and looked around in horror, in case there was an insect flying around. The colonel gave up on her and moved on to Eleanor next, thinking she would maybe be a bit more fun, despite her serious look. She had overheard that conversation, and answered "Raspberry ripple!"

"Remember me, my dear?" Tomkin asked cheerily. He hoped she remembered the occasion with Bessie and co, and their subsequent trips with Sergeant Hopper.

"Oh, of course. How could I forget you?" Eleanor smiled sweetly.

Suddenly, Eleanor peered over the colonel's shoulder and thought she could see Dr Roy talking to the lady at the next table. She peered through her lorgnette. Oh no, it was indeed the Doc!

The colonel leaned forward.

"How would you like to be tied to the bed with parachute silk?" He said in a low voice, knowing that she would know about the parachutes.

Eleanor didn't want Dr Roy to hear this conversation. Quick as a flash, she pretended to mishear.

"I wouldn't mind being plied with arrowroot biscuits and milk before bed."

However, it would not have mattered. Dr Roy's hearing aid battery had gone in the one ear, and he hadn't yet got a replacement for it. The lady he was with, Bessie, asked him if he minded helping with the shopping.

"NO," he replied angrily."I don't believe in wife swapping. If you have a husband, you shouldn't be here. I most certainly don't have a wife."

At that moment he caught sight of Eleanor. In truth, he hadn't purposely come to the speed dating. He had popped round to see her, found her not at home, and asked her neighbour where she was. "She's at the Quaker Hall" was the answer. Dr Roy thought that was odd; what would she be doing there? Imagine his surprise when he got there and saw the sign!

It was time to face the music! Dr Roy was coming round to her table next.

"Well, Miss Kyson-Pointer, you have some explaining to do!"

"Please don't be cross with me. I only came here to see if I could find someone to ride the tandem with me."

"You want to find someone randomly? That's not like you at all, Eleanor."

"NO!" shouted Eleanor. "I said someone to ride a tandem!"

"But *I* will!" shouted the Doc, finally grasping what she was saying. "I'm a bit nervous, but we can practise in the park."

So Eleanor ticked gentleman thirteen on her list, and at the end of the evening there were only two matches announced by the lady in "Country Casuals." Eleanor and Roy were one, and Doreen had been found to match a lovely chap with whom she used to go to school.

Eleanor and Dr Roy walked home together.

"So we're a match!" announced Eleanor, who was very embarrassed.

"There's a catch?" misheard Roy."What is it?"

"No, you're a good catch!" she laughed.

What about poor Colonel Tomkin and Les? Cedric was too rude for the elderly ladies of the town, but Les and Bessie became very good friends.

The GP Pilot Scheme

Eleanor had been feeling under the weather for some time, and Dr Roy (who was not a doctor of medicine) suggested going to see the GP. On arrival at the local surgery there was a banner on the wall saying

GP Access Pilot Scheme.

(The sign was meant to read "Extended GP Access pilot" but the first word had been scrawled over with an indelible pen).

"What on earth d'you think that means?" Roy asked Eleanor, hoping to cheer her up. "D'you think they're so short of GPs now they are training pilots to do a few more years and convert?"

"I wouldn't be surprised," a young chap sitting near them piped up."Did you know there's more chance of seeing a deer in your garden than seeing a doctor on the day you need to?"

"I can well believe it. I usually see the practice nurse. Mind you, she's very good."

"Maybe GP's and pilots could be interchangeable," suggested a dark haired lady in the corner with a small boy."The Health Service is so short of doctors, nothing would surprise me now."

"Well, we all have a nose, an undercarriage and bowels, like a plane!"

"Well, my propellers are really playing me up today, and my bunions," an elderly lady in the corner announced. Eleanor looked closer and realised it was Bessie, their friend.

"Hello, Bessie," Eleanor said."Sorry to hear about your bunions. Where, exactly are your propellers? That is, if you don't mind my asking."

"Oh, hello, Roy and Eleanor. I was referring to my heart going pitter–pat. Sort of palpitations, really. What's up with you then?"

"I'm feeling under the weather," was the reply, not wanting to go into detail. "But while you're on the subject, we do have quite a bit in common with aeroplanes. We have bones, or a skeleton, like the fuselage of a 'plane, and our arms are like wings, but hopefully not too many of us try to fly. I suppose you could say our feet are like wheels," Eleanor was now getting into the swing of it.

"Well I could do with my feet turning into wheels today, I can assure you."Bessie's feet were really playing her up. "What if our friend Les appeared now, with Hades? D' you think he could be a sniffer dog?"

"He'd be a very good one," Eleanor suggested.

"Thinking of airports, and parts of planes, humans no longer have a tail, and have a coccyx instead, which usually causes lots of pain," added Dr Roy, who suffered a lot with his lower back pain.

"Thinking of pain, I had to have "Voltarol" suppositories after my hip operation", said Bessie. "That was awful. But better than having to swallow tablets."

"As long as you didn't swallow a suppository," said a chap who looked like a soldier."I had a friend in the forces who did that. He reckoned it tasted of soap."

"I think you're thinking more of the suppositories used for constipation", Dr Roy reckoned.

"Oh maybe, as he did spend a long time in the bathroom afterwards," was the reply.

"As you mentioned constipation," muttered an elderly chap. "That's what I'd like to see the doc about. I reckon by the time I see him I will no longer have the problem!"

"Well, we don't all want to hear that thank you," another patient joined in."How about the cockpit then? Is that the brain?"

"Well yes, I suppose so."

"The command and control must be from there" This was the army chap.

Someone then entered the surgery. It was Colonel Tomkin, who was now using a mobility scooter. It was actually the first time he'd used this and he was driving quite quickly, as he had done in his car a year previously, and only just stopped before he knocked into the pushchair belonging to the small boy in the corner. His mother wasn't impressed.

"You need a licence for that thing," she remonstrated. "Or your cockpit needs someone in control."

"Don't you talk about my cockpit like that!" The colonel's monocle popped out of his left eye. "I lost my driving licence and I will jolly well keep using this. If not I'll be trapped at home!" The receptionist looked up from her computer and signalled with a finger to her lips for the patients to be quiet, her face furious.

Someone then came out of Dr Platt's office. It was a beaming middle-aged gentleman. "Well," he announced to the waiting room. "We may have a solution to my snoring problem. Mrs Philips may soon manage a good night's sleep!"

Everyone sighed with relief that at least the next person in the queue was able to go through.

"Mr Smith, please, "the Doctor came and beckoned to the young man who mentioned deer.

"Don't worry," he joked to the waiting patients, by now similar to a stand-up comedy audience."I'll make sure I see his pilot licence, before I tell him about the spots on my posterior."

Just at that moment Doreen, a friend who lived in the Colonel's block of flats, walked in.

"Hello Doreen, welcome to the chaotic airport waiting area!"

"Is that what you call it! Well, I need to go straight to the baggage carousel, as I've lost some of my baggage," Doreen said wistfully. Indeed she did look even slimmer than when Eleanor had last seen her. She didn't like to be rude though, and said "It's good to offload emotional baggage, my dear."

It was very hot in the surgery and a rather more friendly receptionist was offering the patients

water from a large plastic water container. Dr Roy passed a plastic cup of water to Eleanor, and then passed one along to the Colonel.

"Thank you," said Eleanor. "We all need water and fuel, like a 'plane. They'll be needing to serve up snacks here soon," she observed."Some people will have been here almost an hour, and will have forgotten what they came for." The constipated gentleman was then called in to see the locum doctor, and the lady with the little boy was called in to see the lady doctor (who was incidentally Dr Annette Shufflebottom.)The patients then realised the little boy had something in his ear, as his mother signed to them as she walked past. "Gave him some five penny pieces for his money box, and he put one straight in his ear!"

The practice nurse, Helen, then came out to collect her next patient, Bessie. A teenage boy walked out clutching his arm, presumably after an injection of some sort, and was muttering under his breath.

"Wasn't he in there a long time?" muttered Dr Roy to Eleanor.

"I reckon he had needle phobia," muttered the Colonel."Don't blame him. Have the same problem myself, even though I was in the parachute regiment."

"Well I hope you don't have to have a needle today," said Eleanor, trying to sound supportive.

"Oh no, I expect they'll be trying to give me painkillers, which never help," he muttered. My fingers can barely control that vehicle, but I'm refusing to be pushed around in a wheelchair".

"Well, if you have arthritis, there is an injection every so often that can help," Dr Roy piped up, but the Colonel was obviously not listening.

"Eleanor Kyson–Pointer to gate five, please. That is if you wouldn't mind sitting outside my office," Dr Platt's cheery voice was heard in the background. "Many apologies for the delay to your flight."

A Day in the Country

The group of elderly friends had a policeman friend, Sergeant Hopper, who offered to take them for a day trip on his day off in the middle of June. They had a vote on where they'd like to go, and the most popular choice was an unusual little place up in Norfolk. It had lovely gardens with lavender amongst its many bushes, an old house dating back to Georgian times, a maze, and even though it was situated near the Broads it had its own ornamental lake, so there was to be a trip on the swan pedaloes, with Hopper and a staff member helping with the pedalling.

Well, Hopper didn't bring his driving gloves on this occasion, but a professional–looking peaked cap. He had a very round red face, and was altogether quite a round chap. Today he was wearing a pair of knee–length striped shorts, which made him look like an overgrown schoolboy. He had a seven-seater vehicle in which he used to transport his four children, but as teenagers they were now getting too old to be seen in dad's car unless it was to go "night-clubbing".

First he collected Doreen and Les from the warden–controlled flats, with Hades the helping dog of course. He had offered to take Colonel Tomkin, but as this gentleman was now mainly using his mobility scooter, and he had nearly tipped out of it on a hillock in the local park (and called a laughing bystander a "pillock"), he'd decided not to go. He did however hand over seven life jackets from his days in the parachute regiment, as he knew about the trip on the swan pedaloes. Bessie and Cuthbert were then collected from their respective homes, and finally Eleanor and Dr Roy were the last two to be picked up from the other side of town. Everyone brought hats and sunscreen, and long sleeved clothing in case it got cooler, especially on the boats.

They arrived at Bushkin Manor soon after eleven and piled into the cafeteria for coffee and biscuits. They then split into two groups, with Eleanor, Roy and Cuthbert looking around the mansion, and the others together with Hopper went to see if they could find their way round the maze. Bessie was still suffering with her bunions so sat on a bench near the beginning of the maze.

The friends had a toasted sandwich lunch together in the conservatory building which had been added on and was a lovely place to soak up the sun. The sunscreen was then liberally applied to arms and necks. The pedalo boat rides were booked for two thirty. A member of staff was to help Doreen, Les and Cuthbert into one swan boat and Hopper was to help Bessie, Eleanor and Dr Roy into another. They all lined up by the side of the lake and put on the Colonel's life jackets, which had been deemed safe by the lake authority. It had also been agreed that Hades could be taken in one swan pedalo, with Les of course, but he barked so much at the swan shape that he had to stay on dry land. Luckily he had a collar marked "Helping Dog" so no one worried too much that a large husky was running up and down the side of the lake as everyone got in the pedaloes. At one stage Hades came across a couple of terriers under a tree. He peered up the tree where their owner (presumably), a young man, was perched up on one of the branches! At least the dogs were on terra firma!

Well, Hopper helped his three charges into their boat and the two pedaloes set off on a leisurely tour of the calm lake. Hades tried to keep near the one Les was in, running round on the grass, backwards and forwards, eyes fixed on his beloved owner. Doreen and the member of staff (Siegfried) were pedalling this pedalo. The other one was going at a more relaxed pace, with Hopper and Eleanor pedalling. She had had plenty of practice with her bicycle. Les and Cuthbert were trying to play "I-Spy", and getting in a pickle with names of trees and bushes so no one knew what anyone was trying to spell, with Bessie and Dr Roy from the other boat trying to help. The hour trip went by too quickly, and Hades was resting on the grass with only one eye now on his master. The first pedalo came to rest with its rear end parallel with the landing area. The four of them got off; the three friends said goodbye to Siegfried and went to sit on a nearby bench, taking off their life–jackets; then the other boat came to the landing place. Hopper stepped off first so he was able to help the elderly folk. Eleanor stepped over the gap graciously and held Hopper's hand to get to safety. She then held Dr Roy's hand so he could climb over. However, when it came to Bessie's turn, she missed her footing, as her feet were still quite sore, and SPLASH! Into the water between the little boat and the landing stage she went! The pedalo had drifted away a bit, and Bessie was thrashing about with her arms in the rather cold water.

"Help!" she shouted, worrying she would go under. However the Colonel's life jackets were the best ones possible. She couldn't go under the water even if she'd wanted to. By now Hades was barking beside her on the edge of the water, and he jumped in with a splash. The dog had a special rapport with Bessie as she and his master had become good friends. He tried to push her along to the edge with the side of his face, while kicking with all four paws. In the meantime a passer-by had shouted after Siegfried, who rushed back to the water's edge and with the assistance of Dr Roy and Eleanor, dragged Bessie out of the water. They lay her down on the ground, with Siegfried checking her pulse, and people rushed over from the restaurant with blankets for her. Hades had jumped back out again, and as well as shaking himself over everyone around, was licking her face. He knew from his training to be a helping dog that humans had to be a certain temperature, and was certainly trying his best to maintain this. Bessie was breathing, and her heart beating, but she felt very cold. However, more staff members had appeared, and decided to rig up a sort of screen around her before an ambulance arrived. The rest of her friends, led by Hopper, Eleanor and Dr Roy decided to go for a cup of tea until it was decided whether Bessie was fit enough to travel with them or whether she needed checking over in the hospital. She had no other clothes with her, apart from a lightweight jacket, and obviously would have to remove all her wet clothing. Les waited with her, and Hades did of course.

Around five pm Hopper received a message from the ambulance crew that Bessie was to be checked over at the nearest hospital, and would most probably be taken home the following day. Les decided to travel in the ambulance with her, but they weren't keen on having such a wet dog there too. Poor Hades had to travel back in Hopper's vehicle with the others, but he knew everyone quite well now. The group sang a few songs on the way home, but they all worried a little about Bessie. Hopper dropped everyone home, and Hades went to Cuthbert's house for the night. The policeman then went to see Colonel Tomkin and told him about the pedalo trip.

"You must keep me informed," the Colonel barked at Hopper. "Those lifejackets are flippin' marvellous."

"Well, I reckon it was the staff, Hades, Eleanor and Roy, as well as the lifejacket," reckoned the policeman. "I'll let you know when Bessie's home."

Bessie returned by lunchtime the following day, with some rather inelegant second-hand clothes donated by the Hospital League of Friends, together with a pair of gentlemen's enormous sandals she'd been lent. Her own sandals were somewhere in the lake at Bushkin Manor.

"How are you feeling?" asked Eleanor when she went round on her bicycle to see Bessie.

"Well, I feel fine now. It was an awful shock. Would you believe, the best thing is, I now have an appointment to have my bunions looked at!"

"Well, as long as there's something good!" Eleanor didn't really know what to say on the matter.

"Things always happen in threes"

Spring had come round again, and it was time for a spring clean; the elderly folk were making cakes, new clothes, and sorting their gardens, trimming lawns and hedges.

Colonel Tomkin had decided to bake a cake. He wasn't really a "domesticated" sort of person, but he wanted to invite the rest of the "gang" around for a small tipple and a slice of cake. He had a good old sort–out in his cupboard, which was in the hall, and he found out an old mixer from the 60's. He had heard a recipe on the radio for a chocolate courgette cake, and had written down instructions in his own style of shorthand. He put the two beaters onto the hand held device and assembled the ingredients, which he'd bought the previous day. The instructions told him to "whisk the eggs, oil and sugar in a large bowl, and then add the courgettes and vanilla essence". He had to then put the dry ingredients, flour, cinnamon, nutmeg, baking powder, bicarbonate of soda, walnuts and sultanas into another bowl. He then had to stir one into the other, but wasn't sure how to do this bit, so thought he'd call Eleanor, to see if she could give any advice.

"I'm trying to make a cake here, Miss KP," he barked in his military tones. "Is it OK to mix the wet ingredients in with the dry ones, with a cake mixer?"

"Oh yes, I'm quite sure that's fine," she replied. "Fancy you making a cake, I'm quite impressed. I'm just trying to fix a few things with my old sewing machine. I have a year-old pile of mending, with a tablecloth, a skirt to hem, and some small cloths."

"Well, don't forget the tipples and cake at mine, at four pm," Tomkin reminded her.

"I'll be there."

Eleanor returned to her pile of sewing. She got out the sewing machine and threaded it up as her mother and the teachers at school had shown her, and how she'd remembered up until the 70's. The pile of items which needed mending was ready on the table next to the machine. The latter was an old Singer with a foot pedal, so you just had to guide the fabric with your hand. It hadn't been used for quite a few years. She had tacked the tablecloth along the part she wanted to stitch, and put her foot on the pedal. WHOOSH!! The machine seemed to have a mind of its own. It didn't want to sew the items one at a time, as she did, but it decided to do them all in one go. Not content with sewing the uneven hem of the tablecloth, followed by part of the hem of the skirt she wanted to do next, it ran over the pile of cloths and onto the skirt she was wearing at the moment. OUCH! The ring finger on her right hand was the machine's last victim, and it stopped as she took her foot off the pedal and looked at her finger. There was a lot of blood! Eleanor wasn't the sort of person to make a lot of fuss, so she wrapped one of the cloths around her finger, and tried to get herself out of the muddle. She had to cut the skirt she was wearing, but luckily it wasn't one of her new purple ones, and she was changing before going out anyway.

By the time she had put the machine away, changed clothes, which was quite difficult with a cloth wrapped round her finger, a good half an hour had passed. She thought about making a cup of tea but it was now almost half past three, and Dr Roy would be here in a moment, and they had a taxi booked to take them to the Colonel's.

Dr Roy took one look at Eleanor's bandaged finger and wondered if they should go straight to the accident and emergency department, as blood was seeping through the dressing. However, Eleanor thought the Colonel must have had some medical training, and would be able to help. She remembered one occasion when a lady friend of his had fainted, and he had found some old smelling salts and the lady had made a rapid recovery.

On arrival at the Colonel's house, they were ushered into the living room.

"So sorry about the cakes. Disaster," he barked, as he poured them both a glass of wine.

"Whatever happened?" asked Dr Roy.

"Come and see the kitchen," the colonel took them both through to see the ceiling and walls where it looked as though he'd either been testing various colours of paint, including green and brown, or maybe even an army khaki, which had gone everywhere.

"Whatever happened? Are you trying different paints or did you have a food fight?"

"No, no. I rang Eleanor for advice with my chocolate courgette cake, put the beaters back on the mixer, and mixed the wet and dry ingredients. Damned beater wasn't on properly, was it, and look what happened!"

"Never mind, old bean, "said Roy. "We need you to take a look at Eleanor's hand, please; she's had an accident that was even worse, with her sewing machine."

They rushed back into the living room and the Colonel asked if he could look at the offending finger. He unwrapped the "bandage" and immediately started barking orders.

"Roy, in my room, next to this one, first aid box on bedside cabinet, please."Roy had no problems hearing the colonel, luckily.

He went and brought the first aid box. Inside were various items, some of which looked ancient. The colonel fished out a mustard coloured bandage and some antiseptic wipes, a small pair of scissors and a pair of latex gloves. He put on the gloves, opened the wipe packet and cleaned Eleanor's wound. She winced and jumped, but didn't dare make a fuss. He then cut a large piece of bandage into a thin strip, wrapped it around the finger, and fastened it with a safety pin he had also in the box. It smelt of mothballs mixed with mustard.

"We used these on horses when I was in the cavalry regiment. The mustard has healing properties. It's soaked into the bandage."

"Wasn't that years ago though? Over sixty years even?" asked Eleanor, getting rather worried.

By now, the other guests, Bessie and Les, had arrived, with Hades. Bessie had made a large Victoria sponge, so they had that with their wine, or sherry, and a few Garibaldi biscuits the colonel had foraged out when his cake had gone wrong.

"What made you late?" Tomkin questioned Bessie. "I hope it wasn't the cake making."

"No, poor Cuthbert had a bit of a problem this morning. He was mowing the lawn, but he wasn't keeping an eye on the cable, and BANG! It cut out, of course, and he wasn't hurt, but he had quite a shock. Luckily he's bald, or his hair would have stuck up on end!"

They all laughed at this spectacle, and settled down to a game of cards. It later emerged that Cuthbert had then had to borrow the next door neighbour's lawn-mower to finish the lawn, and had then had to go to Bessie's (she was his sister) for lunch, as he didn't fancy having to use any more electrical gadgets that day.

The following day, Eleanor's wound was no longer seeping through the bandage, but it was throbbing a bit. Dr Roy suggested she should go along to see the nurse at the surgery. Helen was available at two o'clock, so they went for a spot of lunch first.

There was a queue at the surgery, as always, and there were some interesting people to chat to, including a lady called Bunty and her gentleman friend Colonel Clutterbuck.

"Miss Kyson-Pointer," Helen called out at almost three o'clock.

"Let me see that finger," she said as Eleanor walked slowly into room six. "Whatever happened?"

"The sewing machine sort of went *wild*," Eleanor said sheepishly.

"Our kind friend the colonel put a sort of mustard poultice on."

Helen had now unravelled the whole bandage and the cut area was healing nicely.

"The mustard poultice has worked very well. No infection, just a clean cut! My congratulations to him! You don't even need antibiotics, just come back next week please."

Dr Roy was very impressed that no more stitches were needed, and the two of them treated the colonel to a more modern cake mixer.

Crime on the Train to Barcelona

It was late October and the group of friends went for a trip to Spain. They didn't fancy flying, as it wasn't good for their blood pressure, so they went by rail and ferry. There were six of them, Eleanor and Roy, Les, Doreen, Bessie and Cuthbert, and of course Les's helping dog Hades came, on his pet passport. Hopper couldn't get time off work to go, but he gave them as much advice as he could and a telephone number, and Colonel Tomkin didn't fancy taking his mobility scooter so he dropped out. They all "travelled light" with one bag each, and Bessie helped carry some food and items for Hades.

Well, they had to change train in Paris, and travel between two stations there. Roy's daughter had pre-booked a taxi to take them from one to the other. The driver met them with a placard with "The Six Intrepid ones" (in French) and took them to Austerlitz station. Here, a glamorous lady showed them to their seats and they settled down to have a siesta, as they were exhausted.

All of a sudden Doreen overheard a very worrying conversation, in English.

"When I give this sign," a red-haired lady muttered to her older male companion, miming shooting with her two fingers pointing horizontally "you must get up off your seat, walk very slowly from here to the back of the train, find Minako and Froso, and send them to me. Then you must find Hector, and do the deed."

Doreen went to poke Les in the ribs, but he was asleep, his mouth open, Hades at his feet. Dr Roy of course could not hear any of the conversation, even with his hearing aids, and Eleanor was busy reading. She didn't like to shout across to Bessie or her brother Cuthbert, (who were eating Kendal mint cake as though on a trekking expedition), that there was a murder being plotted right under their noses. She got out her notebook and jotted down the three names she'd heard and a description of the red-haired lady.

The gentleman who had been sitting with that lady peered around the carriage suspiciously before ambling slowly through to the next carriage. Doreen was shocked. Should she tell someone a murder was being planned? Why were they not speaking French? Mind you, it isn't good to be speaking English or French if you're planning a murder in a public place.

Hades seemed to be restless; maybe she should walk him towards the back of the train? She asked Les if he would watch her bags, as well as all the others', and said she was going to find out where the conveniences, and refreshments, were to be found.

On her way to the next carriage she saw a lot of ladies coming towards her. Could any of them be Minako or Froso? She hurried along to the next carriage and through to the end one. She peered around for a gentleman who may have been killed. There in the furthest carriage of the train was a body, slumped across the double seats with his legs dangling. Doreen gasped. Should she touch him? There was no blood, and she couldn't see his face. She must go and find a guard. Surely, if he were dead, Hades would raise the alarm, as he was used to checking body temperatures. The dog did however look as though he needed to "spend a penny", so Doreen thought it best to ask a guard. This chap was to be found even further towards the back end of the train.

The guard sat down a very agitated Doreen, trying a bit of French mixed with sign language, and assured her the train would stop in a minute and Hades could have his comfort break, and then he would accompany them both to see the gentleman concerned.

Alas, when Doreen and the guard returned to the last carriage, the body was no longer there! Had it been moved? Had he been asleep? Meekly Doreen apologised and went back to her carriage, muttering to the dog, "I'm sure there was a body slumped there earlier."The guard gestured and told her in broken English that he would soon be checking tickets, and everyone would have to be in their places eventually.

She sped back to the carriage to her companions. Most of them were awake now, and wondering where she'd been.

"I think there may have been a murder committed on the train!" she whispered as loudly as she could to Eleanor and Dr Roy.

"A birder?" exclaimed Dr Roy, who had taken his hearing aids out for safe–keeping. "Is there a bird watching group on the train? Do they have any bino..."

"No, a murder!" Doreen snapped. "And, to top it all, the body has vanished." Eleanor and Roy looked over to where the red-haired lady was surrounded by people. "Minako and Froso, where's Hector?" a huge man sounding like a policeman barked at a very petite, possibly Japanese lady, and an elegantly presented lady who could have been of Mediterranean or Greek origin.

"He was with us in the last carriage," the Japanese lady replied, in very good English."Then Andy came to find us, and that's all I know."

"Well, hadn't you best try and find him?" asked a possible policeman."Who saw him last?"

"I did!" a voice piped up. Doreen was sure this was the voice of the chap who had been asked to "do the deed."

"What was he doing?"

"He was singing a famous song from the seventies when I saw him," came the reply."I think it was *Waterloo*."

Just then the guard arrived in the carriage and asked in French and English for everyone's tickets.

"How many people in your group?" he questioned the red-haired lady in a strong French accent.

"There're ten of us."

"Where is the person sitting 'ere?"he gestured to an empty seat. Was that the seat that belonged to the "dead" man?

"Ah, he's bringing refreshments," said the lady who may have been "Froso".

"I need to find 'im," the guard said, coming closer to check Doreen and her companions' tickets.

He then moved on to check the tickets of a young couple. At that moment, a chap strode into the carriage rustling a carrier bag which appeared full of baguettes and crisps.

"Here he is!"called "Red-hair" to the guard.

"Splendide!" declared the latter. He went over to wink at Doreen."No-one is dead, I 'ope."

The red-haired lady's companion heard this.

"Well we're doing a murder mystery weekend in Barcelona, and we had a trial run. Sorry if we alarmed you!"

A lesson in Spanish

The friends arrived at their destination, a small hotel on the coast not far from Barcelona. The hotel was called the "Pensión Flamenco Rosado", which had made them all giggle."Ooh, is it a pension because it's for pensioners?" Doreen had asked. "No, eet ees *Espanish* for a little 'otel," the gentleman at the desk, with a purple shirt, and a thick, dark beard, had replied. He handed over the keys to the group."You don't usually 'ave a dining room in a pensión, but we do 'ere."

"How about the Flamenco Rosado?" Eleanor wanted to know. She was regretting that she hadn't learnt some Spanish when she was younger. Dr Roy and Les had learnt a bit of Spanish years ago; Les came over to Benidorm in the seventies before it became very popular.

"Eet ees a pink bird with long legs like a stork, or even a Flamencan gentleman who has a pink face, per'aps." He grinned at this, and Doreen muttered, "I think the bird he means is a flamingo."

Les and Hades shared a room, and Bessie and Doreen shared one, Doctor Roy shared with Cuthbert, and Eleanor had her own room. There was a view of the bay to each room and an en-suite bathroom. They all had a good afternoon "siesta", as they hadn't slept well on the train, especially after the worry of the murder.

They met in the dining room at seven thirty when dinner was served. There was an assortment of staff members bustling around in black uniforms; the ladies wore white aprons over theirs. A long table was laid out with various choices of food. They each collected a tray and moved along the table. Bessie went up twice, once to collect her own and once for Les. He waited at the table with Hades, who had his own biscuits. He only needed to eat one meal a day as huskies don't eat a huge amount. He chatted to a group of Danish young people who were backpacking around Spain.

"Tortilla?" a gentleman with wispy hair and greying sideburns asked Cuthbert, pointing to a wonderful yellow creation, a perfect disc in the base of a pan.

"Is that a turtle?" Cuthbert asked Dr Roy. "I didn't know they ate turtle in Spain."

Doctor Roy didn't hear properly, and wondered why Cuthbert was mentioning Myrtle, his wife who had passed away many years previously.

"Don't be silly," Eleanor piped up. "It's a lovely omelette. The Spanish make a wonderful one with potato and onion." She said this last bit loudly so Doctor Roy could hear. Cuthbert nodded in acceptance to the slice offered.

"Pan?" the gentleman asked, when Cuthbert's plate had a large slice of omelette on.

"Why would I want the omelette pan?" Cuthbert asked. The others now had slices of omelette too, and could see that the gentleman was offering Cuthbert bread from the hunks of gorgeous home–baked baguette. "Pan" must be the word for bread! It looked a bit crusty to Eleanor, who had a few dentures, and to Doreen, so they opted for "patatas bravas" instead, wondering why the potatoes were described as "brave".

When Bessie went up for her own meal, having delivered Cuthbert's, there seemed to be a steaming hot dish on the table. "Macarrones?" a lady with a chef's hat and a lot of make-up asked her.

"I'll have a macaroon after, please..."she began, and then realised the lady meant the hot pasta dish. "I'm so sorry. Yes, I'd love some macaroni."

Everyone else then had a portion of the lovely macaroni cheese too, and despite the "brave" potatoes being fiery, the meal was enjoyed by all. They could only manage grapes and yoghurt for dessert, even though the desserts looked lovely. At one stage Doctor Roy saw a large piece of cake being taken over to someone, and said to Eleanor "What a lovely looking gateau." The waiter looked around in alarm, muttering "Gato?" Les then remembered that "gato" is Spanish for cat, and they all had a laugh at this, amused that the waiter thought they'd seen a cat in the dining room. They tried to have a chat to some other guests, the Danish group, "The Explorers" as Doctor Roy called them. They then turned in for the night and all slept like logs.

The following day, the group of friends had a lie in followed by a breakfast of croissants and coffee, although Cuthbert and Les chose bacon and egg.

They set off outside in the bright sunlight, with fans and sunglasses, and a couple of umbrellas to use as sun-shades. They sat down on a bench in the middle of the beautiful town, by a clock tower, watching people bustling in the market. There were young men, some of whom were smoking and laughing flirtatiously with the ladies. There was a group of older gentlemen drinking coffee and playing card games outside a café, and ladies walking by were talking at the top of their voices in a language that sounded very excited and happy.

All of a sudden Doreen looked over to the far corner of the street. "Ooh, I've seen a ferret shop, and a parakeet shop," she remarked.

"Are you sure?" asked Dr Roy. "It isn't all one pet shop?"

"No, it definitely says FERRETERIA and PERRUQUERIA" Doreen read out the two words very slowly, pronouncing the end of each word as "area". Les then remembered his days learning Spanish, and laughed. "That's an ironmonger and a hairdresser, Doreen. You put the emphasis on the "i". She whipped out a little notebook from her handbag, and wrote this down, adding it to the words she had learnt yesterday evening.

"I suppose you think the "Ferrocarril" is a ferret carrier," laughed Doctor Roy, remembering now the words from years ago.

"No, I suppose it's something to do with iron," Doreen retorted. "Go on, then. I know you're desperate to tell me."

"It's the railway line. I expect it's sort of iron rails," Doctor Roy explained.

"Clever Clogs!"

"Let's go and have a look in the market, and see if we can buy some fruit," said Les, worried the change of water was affecting his bathroom habits. Even though there was fruit at breakfast and dinner, he fancied some more during the day.

Bessie and Cuthbert stayed behind, and the others went to the few stalls they could see in the distance. A large sign read "ROPA REBAJADA".

"Who on earth would want to buy reduced rope?" asked Doreen.

"Well, you never know," laughed Eleanor."You might want skipping ropes for a girls' school. Anyway, I reckon *ropa* means clothes, does it,

Roy?"She had spotted all manner of trousers and shirts, for both sexes, and sequinned tops and dresses for ladies and children, or indeed for whoever fancied them.

"You've got it! Although the idea of lowered rope is quite funny," laughed Doctor Roy.

"Ooh, look," said Doreen. "There are some pears and peaches. How do I ask for six?"

"Seis,"

"Seis pechos, and -er, seis perros," Doreen asked of the gentleman behind the stall, a handsome olive–skinned gentleman with an interesting haircut.

At this, the gentleman began to laugh. Doctor Roy looked extremely embarrassed.

"Pecho is chest!" he hissed at Doreen, very loudly. The gentleman was holding up apricots, bananas, apples, and Doreen pointed madly at the peaches and pears.

"Peras" said Mr Haircut, holding up a pear and putting six in a paper bag. "Melocotónes,"(Me-low-cot-tonnays) holding up a peach and placing six in another. He then said "Perro," pointing to Hades, who was sniffing the air in case there was a meat stall nearby. The gentleman realised Doctor Roy had already explained *pecho* so didn't need to try to demonstrate!

The group went back to find their companions and each enjoyed a piece of fruit. They then fancied a short stroll. In the town, which wasn't far away, they spotted a shop that looked like an optician, which said "lentillas" on the window. Bessie had a laugh at lentils being in the glasses instead of lenses, and they pondered on whether Eleanor could have got a lorgnette made in Spain, and indeed whether they would have tested hearing or made Doctor Roy some special shell aids. Cuthbert looked up the Spanish for lorgnette in his dictionary and found "impertinentes" which made them all giggle.

Doreen then spotted a large building with "BOMBEROS" in large letters on the front, which looked very much like a fire station, and she thought it odd that the word resembled "Bombers."

"Spanish is certainly giving us a few laughs. I wonder if Spanish people find our words amusing when translated to theirs?" They agreed that this must be the case.

They went in a couple of shops to find gifts for their families, and the colonel, and thought "cosas" were tea cosies rather than "things", and all they bought in the end were some tea towels and notebooks!

The group immensely enjoyed the trip to Spain, and by the end of the few days they were asking people how they were and where they lived, and trying to understand the answers!

Even more unusual gifts

There was a bump, and then a scrape. It sounded as though the windows were being rattled, or someone was coming into the house, at the very least. Should she get out of bed, or hide under the covers? Eleanor sat up in bed, and switched on the bedside lamp. The noise seemed to have stopped. Had she frightened a burglar? She put on her dressing-gown.

"Mee-ow," a plaintive voice seemed to say outside the bedroom door.

"Poppet, was that you making all that noise?"

An even louder meow filled the quiet house, and then it sounded as though an object was being bumped against the bedroom door. Eleanor padded over, saying "I hope you haven't brought me a bird or mouse like you did last summer."

She opened the door, and there sat Poppet with, would you believe, half a cucumber, still in its cellophane wrapper, complete with teeth marks!!Eleanor had to find her lorgnette to check what she'd seen. It was now at the cat's feet, and she looked from her owner to the cucumber.

Eleanor was quite surprised. She liked salad, but this was ridiculous. How on earth had Poppet managed to get that through the cat-flap, and then up the stairs?

Should she mention this bizarre behaviour to her neighbours? No, maybe best not to. She didn't want them to think she and the cat were thieves. They might think she was training the cat to do this, like crazy elderly ladies you read about in the newspaper who train their cats to bring expensive items of jewellery back from people's houses.

It was Eleanor's turn to have a few friends come to eat at hers this particular evening. She had made some currant buns, which had turned out like rock cakes, and some sandwiches.

Dr Roy arrived first, with a bottle of Pimms and some lemonade, with mint, strawberries and everything to stir in. Eleanor told him the story of Poppet and the cucumber, and he had a good laugh. "That was her contribution. It could go in the Pimms or the sandwiches", he joked.

Next Les and Bessie arrived, with Hades of course. Bessie had baked a wonderful Victoria sponge. Colonel Tomkin turned up in his mobility scooter, which he left at the front door, and brought a perfected courgette cake, and Cuthbert brought some soft rolls, some with ham and some with cheese, and a little packet containing some chicken from his roast dinner at the luncheon club, which was for Poppet.

"This courgette cake is splendid," remarked Les as he tucked into a second slice. "That reminds me, how's your hand, Eleanor?"

"Thanks to Cedric, my hand recovered very well, thank you," Eleanor delicately replied. She was a little upset no one was eating her rock buns, but to be honest the guests were worried about breaking their teeth, real or not.

However, by the time everyone left at ten in the evening, some in Sergeant Hopper's car and the colonel in his scooter (which he was a bit wobbly with slightly under the influence of Pimms), Eleanor noticed there were only three rock cakes left. Yes, Les had taken one for Doreen, and a few for the policeman's family, but there had been at least twelve originally. Oh well, worse things happen, she thought, and went to bed after tidying the kitchen a bit.

In the morning, when she went down to the kitchen, there was no sign of Poppet, but a muffin (maybe a blueberry one?) was now sitting on the work surface. It was still in a paper case, and there were no teeth marks this time. There had not been any muffins the previous evening. She tried to have a read of the newspaper, but her lorgnette seemed to be missing. It wasn't on the bedside cabinet, or the bookcase where it sometimes was if she didn't take it to bed with her.

"This is very mysterious," thought Eleanor.

She went out for a ride on her bicycle to the library, to borrow a few books on cat behaviour, to see if she could find an explanation for the cucumber. Hopefully she would be recommended one and not need to read too closely.   As she set off, her neighbour two doors down called her over.

"Hello, Miss Kyson-Pointer!" It was the lady, of the house, who Eleanor only saw very occasionally. "Are you missing any cakes with sultanas in?"

"Funny you should say that, a few of my rock buns did seem to disappear the other evening."

"It's my Matador, the big black cat. He brings them back sometimes. I have to confess, he brought a load of bread rolls, one at a time, from the W.I meeting in the parish hall last year."

 "Oh! He doesn't bring cakes out of yours as well, does he? I had a muffin on my work top, and don't think my friends brought it."

"Very possible," Mrs Pickles said.

Eleanor came home with some books on cats, but hadn't been able to look as closely as she'd liked due to not having her lorgnette and being unable to find the spare one.

She was so deep in thought at lunch time that she ate the chicken that was meant for Poppet, brought by Cuthbert. She hadn't realised when she put it in her sandwich that there was a bit of gravy still on it.

During the evening there was a huge commotion going on near the cat flap. Eleanor went in her nightwear to investigate. Inside the house, tugging at something to get it in through the flap, was Poppet. She opened the door, and there on the outside of the cat-flap was Matador, the huge black cat, trying to pull the item back outside!

"What have you got there?" she asked both cats.

She looked closely, and there, neatly wrapped in an old bread bag, was her lorgnette! She grabbed it from the cats, took it out of the bag, and the arm was still on!

Needless to say, she thanked Mrs Pickles for putting her lorgnette in a sort of cover, and they joked about how more criminal activity was going on under their noses than on Eleanor's train to Barcelona.

The Nature Reserve

After the trip to Barcelona, the group felt rather deflated. It was autumn, and life at home was becoming boring. However, Dr Roy spotted a sign in the supermarket for a day out in Pickling Ford, up in Norfolk. "Bring a picnic lunch and your binoculars" it read. He liked to go bird watching occasionally, and he thought the rest of the gang may like to go too, especially as there was an afternoon tea on the way home with hot scones and drinks. Sergeant Hopper was available that day, and offered to take Colonel Tomkin in his car. Bessie decided to stay behind and look after Hades at Les' house, as dogs weren't allowed at the reserve and anyway she was recovering from her bunion operation. Les went with the others on the coach trip.

Well, they all took something towards a picnic. This consisted of checked thermos flasks from the 1970's, containing tea and coffee, plastic containers of sandwiches, Scotch eggs, pork pies, cakes galore, and packets of fruit. They each had a rain jacket, as it looked like rain, and a pair of binoculars, notebooks, pens, and of course cameras!

The coach collected the first group of people from the leisure centre at 9 o'clock, and stopped at various locations along the way. They reached Pickling Ford at 11.30 and our group met up with the Colonel, Hopper and his wife Linda. As well as his monocle, in one eye, the Colonel had a small pair of binoculars round his neck. He had brought his mobility scooter in Hopper's people carrier, so was able to get around the flat areas of the centre.

"I've already seen a splendid pair of birds in the visitor centre," he announced on meeting his friends, showing them a photograph on his digital camera of two smiling ladies who served in the reception and gift shop.

"Don't be cheeky, now," Eleanor delicately told off the Colonel. "We're looking for a pair of egrets, cranes, and a lesser spotted woodpecker."

They were each handed a list to fill in what they saw and where on the reserve – birds, moths, mammals and reptiles, to be handed in later.

"I'm looking for bitterns, and dragonflies", smiled Doreen."I'd like to see a four spotted chaser."

"I say, is that anything like a whisky chaser?" boomed the Colonel. "I just fancy one."

"You'll have to make do with tea, mate", smiled Hopper.

The friends set off through the side door in the centre, above which was a huge mess which looked like a pile of old sticky papers.

"What on earth's that?" asked Cuthbert, seeing one or two large wasps flying around.

"There's a sign here; it's a hornet's nest, and we shouldn't disturb them," read Doreen.

"I should have kept one of my smoke bombs from back in the day", announced Cedric. "I would have smoked the little buggers right out."

"Oh no," called Mabel, one of the staff members. "Leave them alone; then they won't attack you."

Eleanor, Doreen and Dr Roy, together with Linda, set off walking towards a mill, to see if they could see cranes. A large brown bird flew overhead, and Eleanor thought it was a gull.

"It's a bittern!" shouted Doctor Roy, peering through his binoculars. "Well done for spotting it, even if you did think it's a gull."

Linda and Doreen were deep in discussion about some items the group had seen in Barcelona, and Dr Roy had to ask them to be quiet, as he had heard a crane.

"It's a sort of bugle call". They all listened intently for a few minutes, then a pheasant called.

"Is that what you heard?"asked Linda.

"Oh, maybe that's what it was," a crestfallen Roy muttered.

Meanwhile, Cuthbert, Les, Hopper and the Colonel were keeping their eyes on a video recording in one of the hides.

"I think the camera's on a wigeon's nest over there," the policeman pointed out to everyone in the hide.

"Why would we want to come all the way up here to see a pigeon's nest, when we've got 'em all over London?" snapped an angry young man with a Cockney accent.

"A WIGEON, a grey duck with a brown head, it sort of whistles and shakes its tail." Les read from the information in the hide.

"Look, there's a bird called a *shoveler* you can see here, it looks lovely when flying, with quite a few colours." This was Sergeant Hopper, who was beginning to get into the swing of things.

"Did you say shoveler?"piped up the Colonel. "My most recent lady friend, Charlotte, used to shovel her food. That would be a marvellous nickname for her. By the way, I think I've seen a corncrake!"

"That's what you had for breakfast, cornflakes!" laughed Hopper.

The gentleman from London looked over in disgust. "I come out 'ere for some peace and quiet, and all I hear is you!"

"I do beg your pardon, I'm sure." The colonel saluted, and peered through his binoculars. The hide was quiet for another ten minutes, apart from hushed mutterings of "shelduck", "chiffchaff" and "godwit", until Cuthbert announced "Aren't they damselflies over there?" pointing to some blue, fluttery dragonflies hovering over the water.

"Damson flies?" asked Les.

"I don't want those near my home-made jam," muttered the Colonel. On that note the young man stormed out of the hide and banged the wooden door.

They met up for the picnic at one o'clock, sat at outside picnic tables, and compared notes. It turned out that the Colonel had seen more squirrels than birds, but he was going to pretend he'd seen bitterns, as squirrels weren't on the list. Occasionally he got his words mixed round and when telling everyone what he'd seen, he said "Squitterns".

"Is a squittern a wader, a tree-sitter, or an airborne bird?"asked Doreen.

"They nest on the rooftops," announced the colonel with a straight face. He winked at Hopper, who decided to humour him and go along with it.

"They have some squirrel habits, like gathering nuts. I think that what gives them the squits!!"

Eleanor knew they were talking nonsense, and no one else was taking any notice. Cuthbert had looked up into the sky as he thought he could hear thunder, and realised everyone's rain jackets were in the coach, and they were going to have to "make a dash for it". One by one they looked up into the grey sky, which had surely been blue this morning. Spots of rain were starting to fall, and they gradually became a steady downpour. They rushed back towards the visitor centre, Doreen and Eleanor holding on to one another; Cuthbert and Dr Roy carrying the large picnic bag between them. Hopper assisted the Colonel to get his scooter up the ramp and into the visitor centre. Mabel and her colleague helped them pour out the tea into the flask cups, and they waited there for the coach driver to bring the coach nearer, which was easier than finding everyone's rain jackets.

Once everyone was on the coach, Hopper went to find Cedric's rain jacket and his own, and they drove home. Cedric had an old hip flask he had hidden in a compartment of his scooter, and was swigging whisky as he sang as many rude songs from his old regiment days as he could remember. Meanwhile the group on the coach were singing as many songs as they could with birds in the title, including a Beatles one, "Blackbird" and Doreen's favourite singer

Bob Marley's song "Three little birds." The afternoon tea stop went very well, but the colonel didn't join them as he was a little inebriated. By the time they got back to their homes there was a wonderful rainbow. Les looked at the pictures he had taken on his digital camera, and showed them to Bessie, but she couldn't make out a single bird. There was a picture of the hornet's nest, which looked like a sticky pile of paper, and some of arms and legs, and a plate of Scotch eggs and a tartan flask. "Ah well", thought Bessie, "I didn't miss anything very exciting."

The Colonel and his cake

Winter was fast approaching, and the Colonel was getting a lot of pain in his joints from his arthritis. The painkillers from his GP weren't helping him a lot, and his grand-daughter Selena offered to make him an unusual type of Brownie.

"I'll make you some *special* cake," she said with a wink. "But you must *not* have more than one slice at a time."

In the meantime, he had purchased a new mobility scooter with the proceeds from his previous one plus some paintings from his former regiment. The previous vehicle was quite difficult to manoeuvre, but this new one had a hare symbol to the left and a tortoise one to the right, with a simple lever in the middle, to control speed. It also collapsed more easily to fit into a fairly sizeable car.

On Saturday he felt quite poorly, but remembered he had the lovely cake in his fridge. He had a very large slice of it at eleven with his coffee, and felt so tired he had a little sleep. At three in the afternoon he remembered he had to pop into town to do a few mundane things, such as getting milk and bread; not to mention practising driving the new vehicle. He'd also offered to pick up some printed leaflets from the leisure centre for Selena, and he wanted to pop to the fresh fish shop to show the scooter to his daughter who worked there. He had a small second sliver of the cake before he left.

Off he went, at "tortoise" speed, heading towards the leisure centre. The scooter had a horn, which sounded like an indisposed frog, and he pressed that a few times, ensuring a few pedestrians stepped to the side rather rapidly. Once at his destination, he winked at the friendly receptionist, who had been there since the days when the Colonel and his most recent wife played bowls. She opened the barrier and he picked up the swimming and gym times. He then did a three-point turn, (there was, of course, a reverse option too), asked for the barrier to be opened again, turned the lever towards the "hare" and sped out, followed by a group of giggling school girls. The next destination was his favourite café to have a spot of late lunch. As he slurped his soup and buttered a roll, he caught sight of a glamorous lady, maybe ten or fifteen years younger than himself. She had delicately made-up eyes and hair in a long plait down her back. She wore a smart coat over beige linen trousers, and seemed to be just finishing her food.

"I say," he boomed over towards her. "Where did you get that wonderful handbag with a pink flamingo on it? I stayed at a hotel with that ..."

The lady turned to smile sweetly at him, but carried on walking past him to the door. He gulped the rest of his soup, stuffed the roll in his pocket (he hated wasting food) and whizzed out after her. He could just see her in the distance going into a ladies clothes shop called "Adrian Bennett". She herself wanted to get away from the gentleman who had made her feel embarrassed.

The colonel turned his speed back to "tortoise" and followed her into the shop, whistling. It was an old-fashioned sort of place with very good quality brand names such as those in "his day" and changing rooms with old–fashioned chairs and a "Ladies only" sign. The lady seemed to be going right to the back, where the shop extended a long way; the colonel had no idea that such a shop was in the main street. This part seemed to be the lingerie department. Although he was a cheeky chap, he did feel a little uncomfortable about disturbing an unknown lady looking for under-garments.

"Can I help you, Sir?" a large lady boomed at him. "Are you looking for an item for your wife?"

"Er- yes! She rather fancies a silky dressing-gown."

"What sort of size is she?"

The colonel racked his brains to remember a ladies' size.

"...Twelve, I think."

The lady found him a couple, one in a delicate peach shade, and one in pale green. All of a sudden the lady with the pink flamingo bag appeared from the changing rooms, brandishing an armful of clothes. She had been listening to the conversation, and was feeling more comfortable now she thought the colonel had a wife. "I bought the bag here, in fact," she said, tapping it, "as you asked."

"Would you like one for your wife, perhaps? They are good quality, forty pounds at the moment. We still have a few." The large assistant draped the silky gowns over the colonel's lap, and set off towards the back of the shop for a pink flamingo bag. Colonel Tomkin was now beginning to worry he would end up buying lots of items he didn't really want; they were quite expensive at that, and thought he would beat a hasty retreat. He looked through his monocle at his watch, switched the lever down to reverse:- "I'm so sorry, ladies, must dash before the fish shop closes,"- and with that, he revved up to hare speed again and whizzed off. However it was not easy to negotiate the gaps in this shop, and he went flying into a display of fascinators, scraping the boxes that held up the display, knocking the articles all over the place, and finishing up, unbeknown to him, with a blue one with feathers on his head at a jaunty angle. He arrived at the front door, threw the silky gowns onto a display of jumpers, muttered "Sorry, everyone", and left the shop.

He zoomed along the pedestrianised road at top speed, a sea of bemused faces turning to watch, adult arms waving and children's fingers pointing towards his head with the blue feathery adornment. He didn't stop until he arrived at the fishmonger's, where he shouted "OY!" and whizzed in. The vehicle came to a halt when it bashed into the counter, startling a gentleman who had just bought a large bag of fish pie mix. His daughter Jemma looked up from the till, spotted the older gent with a scooter, heard him swear loudly and knew immediately it was her father.

"Dad, what on earth are you doing in such a hurry, and what have you got on your head?"

"Oh, I say! Is it an item of ladies' lingerie?"

"No, it looks like part of a bird!"

He colonel felt his head. A strange rounded metal item was perched at the back, partly digging into his shoulder.

"Oh, my giddy aunt!" he exclaimed."I'm not only going to be arrested for damaging the display, but also for stealing. To top it all, I've scraped my new scooter I wanted to show you!"

"What have you been up to?" Jemma came round to hug him, and removed the fascinator. "Maybe this new scooter wasn't such a good idea."

All of a sudden, a very harassed, large lady appeared. She was wearing an "Adrian Bennett" badge.

"Excuse me, Sir. You left our premises with one of our items, and this lady appears to now have it." She didn't like to accuse such an elderly gentleman of passing on stolen goods.

"I'm extremely sorry, madam. It wasn't quite what my wife wanted. I hadn't intended to bring it out of the shop, but it sort of travelled with me."

"Wife?" asked Jemma. The colonel tried to wink at her, to stop any more mention of the imaginary wife. Luckily she realised, and carried on:- "If my father has caused any trouble, I'm happy to help sort it. Are you going to press charges?"

"Well, our central display has been knocked, but there isn't a lot of damage. We won't press charges under the circumstances."

"I'll come and pick it up for you. I used to do interior décor as a career."

The lady from Adrian Bennett did not fancy anyone in an overall smelling of fish anywhere near the shop, let alone the central display, and she stepped back in horror.

"That would not be necessary, but thank you for your offer. It was purely an accident. Perhaps your mother could come herself and choose some apparel in future. We would be most happy to help." With that, she took the fascinator and strutted off, almost tripping in her high heels, leaving Cedric and his daughter splitting their sides laughing.

The colonel set off home soon after that, and who should he see coming along the street? Yes, it was Sergeant Hopper, in plain clothes. He listened patiently as Cedric told him the story, including how he had a second slice of the cake before leaving the house. They had a laugh about his being "one slice over the limit" and about him having the illegal cake. On Monday the policeman went in his uniform to "Adrian Bennett" and apologised for his friend's behaviour, explaining that his pain medication hadn't suited him. Eleanor accompanied him to help the manager to sort the central display, and she bought a pair of purple pompom slippers from the sale basket. Although she disapproved of what he'd been up to, she agreed that he "had a good heart", and said it was "a sign he had a young mind, still having an eye for the ladies."

If you have enjoyed this book, I would be grateful if you could visit Amazon and leave a review.

Thank you.

35224568R00114

Printed in Poland
by Amazon Fulfillment
Poland Sp. z o.o., Wrocław